# An Ebbing Tide

First published 2006 by Marine Arts Publications.
'Seascape'
King Street
Robin Hood's Bay
North Yorkshire, England. YO22 4SH


ISBN 0-9516184-9-0
An Ebbing Tide.


Reproduction by
Redpress
14 Queen Street
Redcar
North Yorkshire
TS10 1AE

Cover illustration; Robin Hood's Bay,
Steel engraving by Edward Finden circa 1825

# An Ebbing Tide

Sequel to

'For a Keg of Good Brandy'

*Best wishes*

*Pat Labistour*

## Patricia Labistour

MARINE ARTS PUBLICATIONS

*For Cath, Mat and Anna*

This story is dedicated to the now unknown
fishermen of Robin Hoods's Bay
who perished within sight of home
on 14 April 1815,
and to all others lost in the cause of survival.

Also by the same author:

A Rum Do! Smuggling in 18$^{th}$ century Robin Hood's Bay
Lady Mary's Journal (with Mary Neads)
Making Ships in Bottles (with Leon Labistour)

and
the first book in this series
For a Keg of Good Brandy ...

The author has lived in an old sea captain's house dating
from 1824 in Robin Hood's Bay since 1967. She is an
experienced local historian and lecturer, holding a
Certificate in Regional Maritime Studies.

# Preface

Five years have passed since the ending of the first story - 'For a Keg of Good Brandy'.

Conditions in the North Yorkshire fishing village of Robin Hood's Bay are changing, and on his return, Reuben has to remake his life. His experiences during his five years as a convict aboard the government frigate 'Pelican' have taken their toll, and his homecoming is not easy for him or his family. The gradual unpacking of his kit bag, and the stories associated with its contents, which he shares with his wife and son, help him to put the past behind him and look towards his future.

Reuben finds that circumstances forged by history have created a new way of life for the village and its people.

In early days, a basic income was gained through a combination of fishing and small farming; during the height of the smuggling era, the village turned to making a good living through illegal and dangerous means. Now, with the Napoleonic Wars at an end, the Government's need to raise a large amount of tax through the import of luxury goods to finance the naval defences to protect the country from invasion was reduced. Smugglers found the hitherto bountiful profits greatly lessened; the chances of being caught greater than before, as the number of the Preventive men increased as the navy was reduced in strength and employment needed for the many capable seamen no longer required for the defence of the country.

The local population therefore, gradually returned to fishing as their main source of income. They developed the use of the 'five-man boats' which enabled larger catches to be made, and forays further out to sea, being away from home from Monday morning to Friday evening. Although more profitable, the dangers were great, as this story will tell.

An incident which took place on 14 April 1815, when five five-man boats capsized within sight of home, has inspired the ending to this story.

In 1817 there were thirty-eight small cobles and five larger boats fishing out of the village. Gradually, as the old census returns show, many of the old Bay families moved their boats to Whitby to operate from a harbour. Those left behind in Robin Hood's Bay became fewer and more aged as the years went by. By the end of the nineteenth century there were only eight active fishermen left, two of which were eighty-three and eighty-five years old! For many of the old established families, and ultimately for the village itself, the tide was on the ebb.

There were several naval vessels named *Pelican* in the 18th and early 19th centuries. Many of these had eventful voyages. Historic licence has been taken by attributing several of these to the frigate on which Reuben was serving his sentence, but all events recorded in Reuben's story- telling episodes did actually take place.

The list of equipment required for kitting out a Midshipman in the 18th century is authentic.

As in 'For a Keg of Good Brandy', most of the main characters are again fictitious, although they do bear both Christian and surnames common in the village at the time. The Revenue Officers Peter Maxwell and Horatio Roberts did exist and were active in the village during the eighteenth century. There is evidence to support the existence of the mysterious Jiddy Vardy. It is believed that she eventually married one of the uniformed officers and left the area. Although her relationship with Peter Maxwell is supposition, the outcome is left for the reader to decide.

William and Mary Cobb were two of the village grocers. William must have changed his bad habits, for only a few years after the event described on page 60 took place, his name and signature appear on a document appointing him as one of the new Wesleyan Chapel Trustees! After William's death, Mary Cobb donated the land of her small rear garden and 'pig cote' for the Chapel extension building. Captain John Clarke Searle and Captain G. McKinley both commanded the *Pelican* at different times, but the unpleasant Mate Mr. Adams is fictitious, though undoubtedly representative of many of his contemporaries. Reuben's friend, William Young, master's mate, was killed at the moment of victory on the boarding of the American privateer brig.

The stone lined hiding chamber in the private grounds of Thorpe Hall, former home of John Farsyde is still in existence, as is the signalling rock on the battlements of the Raven Hall Hotel, former home of the famous Doctor Willis, both of whom were active leaders in the eighteenth century smuggling syndicates.

Many of the old Robin Hood's Bay cottages still preserve their own secrets of those bygone days...

The cover illustration is a steel engraving of Robin Hood's Bay by Edward Finden, from 'Ports and Harbours of Great Britain' circa 1825. In the foreground are a number of the five-man boats, as featured in this story. Finden was a topographical artist, so we can take his depictions as being reasonably accurate.

Patricia Labistour
Robin Hood's Bay
2006.

# Part One

# The Homecoming

Damaris stood on the slipway to the shore, shielding her eyes with her hand as she looked towards the horizon. The bright sun danced off the waves with a dazzling intensity. Screwing up her eyes against the almost painful brightness she could see, breaking the line between sea and sky, the tall masts of a large sailing ship. Until she could recognise the shape of the hull she could not be certain that this was the *Pelican*, the Government frigate to which her lover, Reuben, had been committed for punishment after being convicted of smuggling.

As the ship drew nearer and Damaris was sure, her heart thumped with anticipation, although it would be at least another three days before the *Pelican* docked in Newcastle and Reuben found his way back to Robin Hood's Bay. Untying the shabby and threadbare scarlet kerchief which she wore around her neck, she waved it excitedly, in the hope that Reuben was looking out for her and would see her waiting for him, standing as she had been five years ago when he was taken from her.

This time, though, she was as happy as she had once been sad. The neckerchief, Reuben's last gift to her, sent from his prison cell, was now ragged and faded and his roughly pencilled message 'I love you, Dam. Wait for me. Reub,' had long-since been fingered away. Damaris had vowed to wear it every day until he returned.

On board the *Pelican*, as she sailed within sight of the village, Reuben raised the telescope to his eyes, hoping that Damaris would be waiting for him. Sure enough, there on the slipway was a female figure, and yes, she was waving a red kerchief. But what was that she was holding? He adjusted the lens and focussed more clearly. By Damaris' side stood a small chunky child, jumping up and down and waving excitedly. Reub lowered the telescope and wondered. Had Damaris waited for him, or was she married to someone else? But, he reasoned, if she was someone else's wife she would not be standing waiting on the slipway, nor would she still be wearing his red neckerchief. He recalled the anguish with which he had written that message to her so long ago from his prison cell, before being taken in chains to his allotted ship. He was also incredibly touched that she was still wearing it. Her feeling for him must still be strong and that gave him comfort and confidence. Reub had worried so much about her, hoping she was alright, as he recalled her irrational behaviour on the night of Hallowe'en that had led indirectly to his capture.

There was only one answer. She was well, and she was still his. Reuben's heart swelled with emotion, as he realised he was coming home - and it looked as though he was coming home to a son!

Five years was a long time to be away. Many tides had ebbed and flowed since he had stood trial at the York Assizes, and heard the dreaded conviction issuing from the stern mouth of the unforgiving judge. It could have been worse, he reflected philosophically. He might have been deported to the other side of the world, and never seen Damaris or his beloved Robin Hood's Bay ever again.

His enforced time in the navy, although unwelcome, had been an interesting experience, with his capability as a seaman instantly recognised by the officers on board the *Pelican*. Even though he was theoretically a convict, his ability and willingness to obey orders soon brought him a measure of respect. All too often, the shortfall in naval crews was made up from the 'prison quota' - a simple way of emptying the vastly overflowing jails of unwanted and useless criminals, ranging from petty sheep-stealers to hardened murderers. To have one as capable as Reuben on the ship was a relief to all his superiors.

His time on board the *Pelican* had taken him to parts of the world he would never have dreamed of visiting. Even though he had never been allowed shore leave, in case he was tempted to 'run', he had absorbed as much as he could of the atmosphere of these strange lands from the deck and had taken the opportunity to purchase some rare and unusual souvenirs from the bumboat men who pestered the ship whenever she anchored off shore. In his kit-bag he had stowed away many strange and wonderful things, always thinking of Damaris whose blue eyes he imagined opening wide in amazement when he was able to spread his treasures before her.

Now, to be in sight of his home shore, he became impatient with the light wind which merely ruffled the surface of the sea as the *Pelican* swung gently northwards. Oh, for a good blow that would fill her sails and send her racing up the coast!

He carefully replaced his telescope, tucking it safely into his belt, and began the long downward climb from the foretop. Easy to find a foothold in this calm sea - not so easy when the ship was heaving and yawing in all directions. Although nimble of foot, and careful of hand, and keeping to the common-sense rule of 'one hand for yourself and one for the ship', he had, on several occasions, been thrown outwards as he clambered over the cross-trees, and with a sickening lurch missed his footing as he slipped on the greasy and wet tarred ropes. More than one of his unlucky shipmates had found themselves thrown overboard and not all of them had been saved.

The *Pelican,* unlike all the members of her crew, did not seem to be in too much of a hurry to get home. She sailed along in a leisurely fashion, giving the men off watch the chance to lean on the rail and have a smoke. Reuben took out his telescope again to catch the last glimpse of the Bay as his ship sailed pass Ness Point and headed towards Whitby. Soon the familiar headland came into sight, with its abbey and church, its lighthouses and piers leading into the harbour. Reuben was frustrated that he could not have been put ashore here in one of the ship's boats, but on appealing to the First Mate was told in no uncertain terms that his voyage was not yet over. He would be paid off in Newcastle and not before. In annoyance, he turned his back on Whitby and went below to start packing his belongings.

Finally, the *Pelican* changed course and lowered her top sails as she swung into the mouth of the Tyne and slowly headed towards her docking place.

The Captain assembled the crew on deck and ordered the purser to pay off regular crew who had shore leave, and those who had served their term of punishment. Reuben impatiently waited his turn and carefully tied the handful of coins in his shirt-tails. Going below to the mess deck he opened the sea chest which he had shared with two of his mess-mates and carefully stowed all his treasures in his kit-bag.

Taking one last look around the cramped conditions which had been home, if not exactly 'homely', for the past five years, it was almost with an odd sense of regret that he squeezed past the old galley stove on which all his meals had been prepared, and said farewell to the one-legged cook who had struggled valiantly under all conditions to do the best he could with the diet of salt beef, sauerkraut, oatmeal, peas, hard cheese and weevily ships' biscuits. Reuben had forgotten what good home cooking was like, and now began a strong yearning for his mother's tasty stews and suet dumplings. Slapping his best mate on the back and taking a final look round at the hooks where he had slung his hammock, and the table where he had eaten so many unappetising meals, Reuben left the mess deck and climbed up the companionway. The sun shone in a bright blue sky, as if to welcome him home.

He ran down the gangplank, whooping with joy at the feel of freedom. Touching firm land for the first time in five years was an extraordinary sensation and it would be a while before he got used to the feel of it not heaving under his feet. Passers-by on the quayside smiled at the happiness on the young man's face. It was obvious he had been away for a long time, and he showed his delight in the broad smile he bestowed on everybody. This morning all the world was his friend. Joyfully Reuben tossed his sailor's cap high in the air, where a playful gust of wind caught it and sent it spinning into the river. Reuben could not have cared less for its loss. He was home - or nearly home - and he was free!

Heaving his kit-bag onto his shoulder, he jauntily walked with a sailor's rolling gait to the inn from where the mail-coach left for the journey south. The coach would not leave for another couple of hours, so Reuben booked his seat and settled down on a bench outside the harbourside inn to enjoy a pasty and a glass of ale. It was good to sit in the sunshine and watch the shipping.

The weather was decent and Reuben was hardy, so he had saved money by taking a seat on the outside of the coach. He grinned and whistled as the cumbersome vehicle lumbered out of the inn yard, accompanied by the shrill sound of the coachman's horn warning of their departure.

The journey passed quickly and pleasantly enough as Reuben chatted to his fellow travellers, most of whom had never travelled beyond the sea, and Reuben's tales kept them entranced. He was a sociable man, the excitement of going home lent an extra enthusiasm to his conversation, and the miles slipped by most agreeably, with the occasional stops for refreshment at which

Reuben found himself the recipient of many generous offers of food and drink.

As the coach approached the steep descent into Whitby the outside passengers alighted, and the strongest pulled on the ropes that assisted the brakes. Only a couple of very nervous ladies remained inside, risking the chance of an upset rather than spoil their fashionable shoes and dresses on the rough and muddy road. In the distance they could see the welcoming sight of the familiar town with the outline of the abbey standing proud on the headland. Not far to go now.

Safely down the hill, it was with a sense of relief that the passengers climbed back on board, and the coach made good speed for the final miles into the port of Whitby. The coachman sounded his horn with a resounding flourish as the vehicle rattled across the bridge over the harbour and wheeled round into Church Street, the horses anxious, smelling the end of the journey as they finally clattered under the narrow archway into the cobbled yard of the White Horse and Griffin.

The arrival of the mail coach, although a daily event, was always the cause of much excitement. Ostlers ran out to take the reins, small boys clamoured round to assist with the luggage and thus earn a few coppers as the passengers tumbled from the coach and shook themselves, thankful to be safely home and dry without any mishaps and without meeting any highwaymen as they crossed the lonely stretches of moorland. Journeys were always fraught with danger.

Reuben politely refused the offer of a last parting drink, as he was anxious to make a couple of purchases before hiring the horse which would take him the last few miles of his long journey home. Hitching his kit-bag over his shoulder, Reuben walked jauntily out of the inn yard and headed off down the narrow cobbled street. The street ran parallel to the harbour, and through the entrances to the narrow yards between the tall cottages he had glimpses of the shining water. Crab pots were piled in heaps outside the cottage doors, and fishing nets hung to dry. The tide was out, and the smell of the harbour mud mingled with the strong aroma of fish and salty air. He breathed it all in with a great sense of contentment. It was great to be back.

Reuben fingered the coins in his pocket and could not wait to spend them. The hard-earned money now seemed worth it. Both his purchases were for Damaris. He smiled as he entered the haberdasher's, and bought the biggest and brightest red neckerchief in the shop. Trying to delay the transaction with such a good-looking young man, the female assistant fluttered her eyelashes and coyly told Reuben that the blue would suit him so much better than the red. It would match his eyes, perfectly. Her disappointment was clearly evident when he explained it was not for him, but for his girl.

He thanked her courteously, then with a more serious expression, walked the rest of Church Street until he came near the end where the hundred-and-ninety-nine steps led up to the parish church of St Mary and the ruins of the ancient abbey high on the cliff above the town. As a youngster he had often climbed the steps, counting as he went, and arriving at a different number every time he went up!

The street was busy, with fishermen loading their catches onto carts, and farm women jostling and shouting their wares, anxious to sell out their butter and eggs before the end of the day. Reuben was frequently delayed by old acquaintances spotting him and congratulating him on his return. He did not want to appear churlish, but pushed them away with a grin, and told them he'd meet up later, but just now he was on an important errand. Weaving his way through the busy street, he finally came to one of the many jet workshops for which Whitby later became world famous. He bent his head as he entered though the narrow doorway, lowered his bulky kit-bag to the ground and shyly asked to see some jewellery.

He knew Damaris had not been much of a one for fancy things, but he wanted to take her something special as a token of his love and as a celebration of his homecoming. His rough fingers felt clumsy as he handled the delicate and beautifully carved brooches and pendants, finally choosing a small oval with a rope edge, in the centre of which lay a small fully open rose. This, he instinctively felt, epitomised his thoughts of Damaris.

He had left her, an unopened flower, but now, with his son at her side, she must surely be a Yorkshire rose at the height of its open beauty. The fine silver chain shone against the dense black of the jet and he thrilled at the thought of fastening it round Damaris' warm neck.

It was a perfect gift, and as the craftsman placed it in a small leather box, Reuben counted out a precious part of his wages. It was expensive, but it was worth every penny. As he felt at that moment, nothing was too good for the beautiful girl who was waiting for him only a few miles away.

Pocketing the box carefully, Reuben took leave of the shop, quietly closing the door behind him, and leaning against it for a moment to reflect on the true meaning of his special gift. His purchases made and safely stowed, all that remained was to return to the coaching inn at the other end of the street, and hire a horse to take him the few remaining miles to his home, and to his love.

## 2

Damaris was fidgety and could not settle to any kind of domestic routine. She was excited, nervous, and apprehensive all at the same time. She could not wait to see Reuben again, yet what if he had changed, and was not the same man who had left her five years ago? His experiences were sure to have had some effect. No matter what he told her of his life during this time, it was so remote from anything she or her family could even begin to imagine. None of them had ever been further than Whitby! Neither had they known anyone other than their close neighbours in this tight-knit village community.

A man with Reuben's experiences behind him would be quite a novelty. He would be in such great demand, with friends clamouring to hear all about them, that he was in danger of becoming a local celebrity. Would he be so wrapped up in his adventures that he would be impatient and have no time for family and the responsibilities of a small child? What kind of people would he have been used to mixing with? Would he be content to go back to the humdrum routine of being a small coble fisherman? Would he be as kind and gentle and loving, or had life among rough men hardened him?

Questions, questions, questions, all waiting to be answered.

Damaris knew that she had changed; she was no longer the young girl he had left behind, whose picture would have remained in his mind. She feared that finding her a mother might be strange and worrying to him.

How could he understand that the girl who had played her Hallowe'en games, and who had faced him, dripping wet, over the amusement of the apple bobbing, could be the mother of his five-year-old son? Only the time of meeting would answer her questions, and deep down she was afraid. Damaris was working herself up into quite a state of panic.

She was anxious also for young Ben. He had been brought up to believe his surname was 'Granger', not his mother's name of Storm. Damaris realised she had maybe been a little presumptuous about this, but by publicly naming Reuben as the father, not only had she found comfort for herself, but also proclaimed to the community that she was proud to be the mother of Reub's child. It put paid to the rumours that, having been called 'Ben' he may have been fathered by Benjamin Rymer. That thought was intolerable.

Gathering courage, she left the house, and taking her young son by the hand, led him up the hill to watch the road down which Reuben would return. The same road that she herself had travelled a lifetime ago, it seemed, when she had foolishly braved the old superstition to watch in the old churchyard at midnight to spy on the procession of the spirits of those who would die during the coming year and had seen the ghostly forms of both Zack and Reuben.

She had fainted with shock, not realising in her emotional state of mind that they were no spirit beings, but living flesh and blood, and were part of that night's smuggling run, where the contraband was being hidden in the old church. At midnight on Hallowe'en, with that scary superstition well believed in, this was as safe a place as any from prying eyes. Her foolishness and fainting had led inadvertently to the capture of Reuben by the local constable, and thus to his conviction and punishment, and for that she would never forgive herself. More worrying, would Reuben ever forgive her?

The events of that long-ago evening which started out as a fun-loving party had, by the early hours of the following morning, had triggered off life-changing circumstances, not only for Reuben, but for the whole of the Storm family, and even Reuben's betrayer, Thomas Duke. Ripples in a pool spread a long way.

There was only one way to find out how things stood between them, and that was to greet him.

Damaris and little Ben climbed the hill and stood for a while watching and listening. At the sound of the approaching horse's hooves she took fright, and dragged her son behind a clump of bushes alongside the path. From there she had a good view of the rider - a tall, fair-haired, broad shouldered young man, with a big grin on his face, and a confident bearing. A neat bundle of clothes was tied to his saddle and over his shoulder he carried a seaman's kit-bag. He whistled as he urged his horse carefully down the hill.

Yes, it was Reuben, but he had changed. His face was tanned and leathery, he looked much older, but his blue eyes still had that irrepressible twinkle that she knew so well. He had grown his fair hair and wore it tied back in a sailor's pigtail. A broad gold hoop glinted in his left ear. My word, thought Damaris, he is handsome! His shoulders were strong and broader than she remembered, and his hands calloused and rough. She felt she would be crushed in his bear-like embrace, and she was scared.

'Is that him?' queried little Ben, peering through the vegetation. Damaris had explained that they were coming out to look for a special visitor, but Ben had not been told who to expect in case things did not turn out alright.

'Yes, that's him!' said Damaris. 'Let him get on his way, and we'll follow in a minute.' She needed to gather her thoughts, then she took her son by the hand, brushed the dead leaves from her skirt, took a deep breath and said, 'Come on then, or he'll be home before we are.'

As he had ridden carefully down the steep hill that led through the village, Reuben had slowed his horse to a gentle walk so that he could take stock of his surroundings. He wondered if the same people lived in the houses he passed, how many had left, or how many of the old people were no longer with them. Which houses now echoed to the sound of new young laughter? Which of his friends had been married - and to whom? There were a number of permutations, and he amused himself by guessing how his friends had actually paired up. Some were almost certainly predictable, but there were sure to be a few surprises as well.

Before making his way to the Storms' cottage, Reub continued his journey through the village, gathering quite a crowd of well-wishers on the way. He leaned from his horse and courteously shook them by the hand, but asked for a few moments of privacy, as he sat at the top of the slipway, gazing out to sea, on the very spot he had observed Damaris waiting for him.

It was time to go, so he slid from the saddle and gave the reins to one of the young boys who had followed him with a gleam of admiration in his eyes which amounted almost to hero-worship. He would have to get used to being something of a celebrity!

He patted the boy on the shoulder, told him to look after the horse, give it a feed and a good rub down, then leave it at the stable of the inn where it would again be for hire.

Turning away from the sea Reuben walked up the familiar alleyway and stood for a moment observing the solid sandstone walls and slate roof, the sparkling clean windows, and the neat curtains blowing gently in the breeze. He took a deep breath, turned the handle of the front door and walked in, wondering what changes he would find.

## 3

Damaris and Ben made their way through the narrow back alleyways and side-streets of the village. It was more private this way, for she was not ready to face the curiosity of the neighbours. Word would have got round that Reuben was coming home, and naturally, the villagers were both inquisitive and anxious. Reub had always been not only a great favourite, but a well-respected man, and his capture and punishment had cast a gloom over the village for quite some time. Damaris had been the recipient of more sympathy than she could deal with, once it became known that she and Reuben were to have married. For a while she had remained in the cottage, not able to face the kindliness of her neighbours.

Outside the cottage door her courage failed her. She opened it a crack, and pushed little Ben inside. She put her ear close to the gap to listen to his reaction. Then, gaining courage, she opened the door a little wider and cautiously peered inside. She smiled at what she saw, and began to feel a little happier.

Ben was feeling a little confused. There was a very big man standing in the room, but he had a kind face and laughing eyes. He was looking around as though it was familiar to him, but yet strange as he had not seen it for five years. What had changed, and more importantly, what was the same? He heard the door creak, turned, and saw a small boy standing hesitantly with his thumb in his mouth.

'Hello! Who are you?' asked the stranger.

'I'm Ben,' replied the child shyly.

'Ben?' thought Reuben to himself. This was a bit of a facer. His heart plummeted as he recalled the womanising Ben Rymer who had caused such havoc at William and Jane's wedding, and whose lecherous reputation was well known. Was this the child of that disreputable rogue and not his after all? The child, however, set his mind at rest quite innocently, as he removed his thumb and lisped through the gap in his teeth.

'Yeth, Ben. Short for Reuben. I'm called after my father. He'th called Reub, and 'coth we can't have two Reubenth, I'm called Ben,' he explained shyly. 'My father'th away at thea. Who are *you*?' he asked.

Reub was wondering how to answer, when the door opened and in came Damaris. After a moment's shyness, she flew into his arms and the five years fled as if they had never been. Little Ben replaced his thumb and watched with studied interest.

The cottage that Reuben had returned to was the home of Damaris' parents, Zachariah and Elizabeth Storm. Reub had been Zack's partner in his fishing boat, and although Reub lived with his widowed mother at the other side of the village, the Storms' cottage was virtually his second home. Here he had watched as Damaris grew from shy child to the attractive girl he realised he had always been in love with, and now, with motherhood, had blossomed into a stunningly beautiful maturity.

Looking round the familiar room, he felt immediately at home, as the well-known furniture and pictures and bits of china all seemed as if they had never moved, and that time had stood still during his absence. Many were the long nights, when even exhausted with the hard work on board ship, Reub could not sleep and whiled away the hours picturing every last stick of furniture in this well-loved room. He knew where every plate stood on the dresser shelves and where every picture hung on the panelled walls. It afforded a great sense of comfort to hope that everything would still be the same. It was, he saw with relief, almost the same as he had left it.

After a while, the door opened again, and Reub realised that time had not stood still after all, for there was a noticeable change in Zack as he came forward with a huge grin on his face, arms outstretched in welcome, and gave Reub a hearty slap on the back.

Zack now had grey streaks in his hair and beard, his face was more rugged and his eyes a little short-sighted. His back was not as straight as it had been, as the rheumatism which was the curse of the fishing community, spending long hours toiling in wet and cold conditions took their toll early, had caught up with him. However, the warmth of his welcome was unchanged as he grasped Reub's hand and thumped him on the shoulder.

'Welcome home, lad! By gum, we're reet glad ti have thee back. Our Damaris has been that miserable.'

Behind Zack stood his wife Elizabeth, still beautiful with her long dark hair, but aged with a sadness in her eyes which she found hard to conceal, even in this joyful moment of greeting.

She opened her arms wide and hugged Reuben as if he was her own son, which, she supposed, in a way he was. Her skin had lost its smoothness and wrinkles gathered at the corner of her mouth and eyes. Whether these were laughter lines or worry lines he did not know. He suspected the latter.

There was a faint but unmistakable scent of fish on her skin. He did not remember that, nor did he remember the roughness and scars on her hands. He raised one to have a closer look, and their eyes met.

'Aye, it's been hard, lad, without thee,' she said softly so that only he would hear, and turned away to surreptitiously brush away an unbidden tear, then turned bravely back to him with her old winning smile. 'Oh Reub!' she said happily. 'It's wonderful to have thee back safe and sound. Now we can be a real family at last.'

'Aye, if Dam'll still have me?' he queried with a sidelong grin at the excited young woman at his side.

'Nay, not much doubt aboot that. Just tek a leuk at 'er!' exclaimed Zack. Reub took a good long look and agreed with her father.

'Now then, young Ben,' said Zack. 'Coom ovver 'ere. This 'andsome young chap is thi faither, who we've told thi aboot. How aboot that! Dost tha like him?' Zack teased.

Ben looked at him thoughtfully for a long time. This was a bit of a surprise, but after a while he trotted over to Reub, put his hand in his and said, 'Yeth, I think I like you. Will you make me a boat and come and sail it with me in the sea?'

'You bet I will,' replied Reub, tousling the curly head. 'Shall we do it timorrer?'

'No,' retorted Ben, tugging at Reub's gansey and jumping up and down with excitement. 'Do it now! Do it now!' It seemed that Reub had been accepted by his small son, so that was one less worry.

'Nay, lad. Be patient. I haven't seen thi mother fer five year. We've a lot ti talk aboot. Be a good lad, and help thi gran, and we'll see thee at tea-time.'

Reluctantly Ben agreed, as Liz grabbed him as he started to follow them. 'Hey, young un, I need some help wi' tea. We've got ti mek some turf cakes. They was Reub's favourite. Coom on, get oot the butter and flour and we'll get busy.'

Young Ben was soon up to his elbows in the flour, and happily wiping his nose on his sleeve, an action Liz preferred not to notice.

## 4

It was a gloriously sunny afternoon, just like the early autumn day when Damaris and Reub had first recognised their love. Gently Reub took her hand and led her away from the curious eyes of the villagers to their favourite spot on the cliff top, from where, hidden in a sheltered hollow, they could look out across the whole sweep of the Bay, yet remain concealed from any unlikely passers by.

The sea was calm and blue as they looked to the horizon, where the fishing cobles were dotted about, busy about their tasks. A soft breeze rustled through the long grasses, creating a wonderful atmosphere of peace and tranquillity.

Cuddled down together in the grassy hollow, they began to make up on some of their lost time of loving. Eventually, contented and blissfully happy, Damaris raised her face to Reuben and said, 'Dost tha know, Reub, how many times Ah've come to this spot and longed to be here with thee? It was so lonely without thee. Ah nivver thowt Ah'd be happy again.'

'Was things that bad, fer thee, ma lass? And Ah knew nowt aboot it. Ah couldna' have borne knowin' and not bein' theer fer thee.'

'Well, it weren't t'best tahm o' me life,' said Damaris, as she went on to explain the confusion in her mind as she first realised what then seemed the awful truth of her pregnancy. Then followed the weeks of nausea and sickness, and the desperation that Reub might not return and she would have to bear the stigma of unmarried motherhood alone. It was not a unique position to be in, but different sections of the community viewed the situation according to their own beliefs and standards.

Damaris was, in a way, fortunate, as she came from a respected family, and her neighbours and friends knew that she was not a flighty girl, and were proud that she stood up for the rights of her forthcoming child. Arabella Clarke, of course, had sniffed accusingly, and looked down her nose but no-one took much notice of her anyway.

The main trouble had come from the vindictive teasing of Ben Rymer, until Zack had given him a good thumping, and when Ben had been born, both Zack and Liz advised she used the surname 'Granger'. There was then no doubt as to the child's paternity, but rumours ran wild in a close-knit community. It was a risk, they knew, but they were all confident of Reub's reaction when he returned.

'But how aboot t'birth itself?' Reub enquired with a worried expression. 'Were it bad?'

'Well, it weren't exactly my idea of fun,' replied Damaris, 'but Liz was wonderful, and Jane Barnard had recently had her first bairn and came and sat with me.' Jennet had wanted to assist at the birth, but Damaris could not bear the thought of her grubby hands prodding and poking. She shuddered at the memory of what might have been. However, Jennet had brewed up some mildly drugging potions which had sent Damaris into a pleasantly woozy state and eased the sharpest of the pangs of childbirth.

'It were quite true, though, Reub. Me ma said Ah'd forget all t'pain and discomfort as soon as Ah held me bairn in me arms. It were wonderful, and Ah'll niver ferget the feel of his little fingers gripping mine, and the puzzled leuk in his eyes as we looked at each other fer t'first tahm. Ah was only sorry that tha was not there ti share it. Tha was that close to me that night, yet tha was miles away and knew nowt aboot thi beautiful little son.'

Reub went very quiet and looked thoughtful, as he tried to remember where he might have been and what he had been doing on the day of his son's birth. Unless something extraordinary happened, one day was much like another on board ship. He found he was incredibly saddened that he did not know.

Damaris brushed away a tear. 'Nivver mind, tha's here now, and we're all together as a family. And,' she added, 'next year tha'll be here to share his birthday! We'll hev a great celebration. This year we can all look forward to Christmas, and a wonderful New Year. That's what matters, what's ahead and not what's behind. Anyroad, eneugh of all that... today the sun's warm, the grass is sweet, and tha's here. Ah can't believe it!'

'Oh, it's true enough,' replied Reub, softly taking her hand and stroking the inside of her wrist with his thumb. She cast her eyes down to hide her feelings as his calloused skin caressed her. He was stuck for words after hearing Damaris telling of the birth of their son. He so wished he could have been there. Emotions ran high and there was a definite lump in his throat. He had to diffuse the situation, or he would burst into tears.

He cleared his throat and spoke in what he hoped was a suitably gruff tone of voice.

'Nah then, let's tek a leuk at thee. What's this scruffy owd bit of rag roond thi neck?' he asked, playfully tugging at the old red neckerchief which had once been round his own neck and had been distinctive enough for it to have identified him to his betrayer. It had been his last gift to Damaris, sent from prison with a message of love roughly pencilled on it.

'Don't tell me tha's still got that owd thing!' he said, touched to the quick that she still wore it. 'Let's be rid of that.'

'No!' Damaris insisted, putting her hand up protectively.

Reub put his hand in his pocket and brought out a small parcel. 'Here then. See what tha thinks o' this.' In the package was the big, bright red kerchief he had bought for her in Whitby. 'It's time tha had a new one. That's reet scruffy.'

'Reet scruffy it might be,' retorted Damaris, 'but it's reet special!' She smiled widely, the smile spreading from her lips right into her blue eyes, which glistened with happy tears.

She told him just how special the old neckerchief was, and how she had felt on the morning that Peter Maxwell had brought it to her, courteously addressing her as 'Miss Storm' and gently laying the package on the table, before retreating silently from the room, leaving her to her grief in private. Her eyes had been red with weeping, as she still felt she was to blame for Reuben's capture. When she opened the parcel and held the neckerchief to her face, the familiar scent of Reuben's skin was just too much for her to bear. She tied it round her neck and vowed that she would wear it every day until he returned, no matter how shabby it became.

Reub was visibly touched as he gently removed the old one and shook out the bright red square which glared in the bright sunshine. Damaris pretended to shield her eyes against its brilliance, but laughed softly as Reub tenderly tied it round her neck.

He neatly folded the old neckerchief into a tidy square and tucked it into Damaris' pocket.

'Keep t'owd one if tha must,' he said, 'but think o' this as a new beginning. We've got ti move on now. We've got little Ben to think aboot. By, he's a grand little chap. Ah knew he was mine t'moment Ah clapped eyes on 'im. Same 'andsome face, same blue eyes, same grand curly 'air ...'

'Aye, and same braggarty nature,' teased Damaris, laughing as he pulled her to her feet, put his arm round her, and led her home to turf cakes and tea.

- 5 -

$T$he Storm family were all sat round the table, laughing and joking. A wonderful aura of happiness hung over them, when suddenly the door burst open and in came Damaris' younger brother, Matt. The laughter was stilled and suddenly the atmosphere changed uneasily. Still in his teens, he had developed into a surly and conceited young man with a disgruntled attitude towards everything and everybody. Slamming the door shut with the heel of his boot, he leaned arrogantly against the doorpost, folded his arms and regarded Reuben with some hostility.

'Oh! So *you're* back then! Mebbe I can git on wi' *my* life now.' He turned to leave as quickly as he had come.

Angrily, Reub got up from the table, grabbed him by the shoulder and spun him round to face him. 'What the hell dost tha mean by that?' he demanded. 'Ah thowt we was mates?'

'We *was*,' retorted Matt, 'until tha was daft enough ti get thisen caught - and all because of 'er,' he gestured roughly towards Damaris.

'Now leuk 'ere. That's quite eneugh. Explain thisen. Ah'm listenin'.'

Reub pushed Matt down into a chair and held him there, before removing his hand and standing back with arms folded.

Matt looked down grumpily, a little ashamed at his behaviour but typically not admitting it.

'Well?' queried Reub. 'What's eating at thee?'

Gradually and reluctantly Matt explained that following Reuben's capture and conviction, Zack had desperately needed his help on his boat, thus putting back Matt's ambitions of studying to go to sea - properly - with hopes of becoming an officer. Ever since Matt had been rescued from the sea after being knocked overboard from the coble during the battle between the Revenue cruisers and the smuggling ship *Kent,* and had ended up being interviewed in the grand cabin of the *Pelican,* he knew that was where he must go. A career as an officer in the Royal Navy would be far preferable to spending his life struggling to make ends meet.

It was a dream that had never left him, and was the only thing that kept him going during the hard and tedious hours baiting lines and mending nets, heaving the heavy cobles in and out of the sea, and for what return? A few miserable fish.

He worked hard, however, and at the end of a long exhausting day he was not much inclined to start poring over books and complicated navigational mathematics, knowing that the chances of being able to use his expertise were not likely to materialise, at least not until Reub came home - if he ever did - and so the resentment built and festered.

Reub, however, understood, and listened until Matt's grumblings slowly subsided. 'Reet, then, that's cleared the air. So, what's tha goin' ti dee abaht it now Ah'm back?'

'Dunno.' Matt shrugged. 'What's t'point? Ah'm jest going ti be stuck 'ere fer t'rest o' me life, like me dad.' He kicked the leg of the chair.

'Oh well, that's that then,' said Reub, returning to the table and resuming his meal. He was not going to labour the point. Let the lad stew.

Whilst Matt was in this truculent mood there was no point in telling him of the plans he had been making for Damaris' brother, to make up in some way for the hardship he had inadvertently brought on the family by his capture.

Word spread like wildfire through the small and tight-knit community that Reuben had returned, safe and sound. His mates were impatiently anxious to welcome him back, but knew his first commitments would be to the Storm family, and then his mother.

They had fewer reservations about disturbing her privacy, as the now elderly Isabella Granger held open house to all her son's friends, so that when he dragged himself away from Damaris to go to his own home, he was not surprised to be overwhelmed with a barrage of cheering and back-slapping that nearly exhausted him. He could hardly see his mother through the roomful of excited fishermen.

In an unusual display of extroverted enthusiasm, he hurled his kit-bag into a corner, leapt up on the table, and whirled around in a fantastic sailor's hornpipe of unadulterated joy. Seeing his mother, eyes alight with pride, hemmed in in her corner, he jumped with the agility of a trained seaman across the heads of his companions and grabbed her in a bear-like hug, swinging her into his arms and burying his face in her now grey hair.

Holding himself away from her, he gazed into her eyes and said, with a guilty apology, 'Ma. Ah've missed thee so much. Forgive me for goin' ti see Damaris afore Ah came across ti thee... but tha knows how it was atween us afore Ah went. Ah had ti see that things was still alreet... and,' he paused with the happiest grin she had ever seen, 'they are!'

Extricating himself from his mother's arms, Reuben turned to his waiting friends. Silas, Sandy and Isaac were the first to pump his hand in welcome, each pressing him for tales of his adventures. "Ere! 'Ang on, lads! Ah've only jest gotten 'ome. Give us a break, for 'eavens sake! It's reet good ti see thee, tha knaws.

Gang along wi' ye ti t'Fisherman's Arms, and Ah'll join thee there. Git me a pint of Richard's best ale, and Ah'll meet thee in a bit. Tha forgets Ah 'aven't seen me old Ma for five years. Ah've things ti tell 'er that ain't for your ears... well, not jest yet,' he added with a grin. 'Now gang along... git o-u-t and Ah'll see thee in a while.'

Reub had dreamed of this meeting during the dark days of his captivity. He had lain in his hammock, conjuring up a picture of Sandy, Silas and Isaac sitting around their favourite table, visualising the empty place that he should have been occupying. Thoughts of home had been very precious, keeping a link no matter how far away he had been at the time. Until then, he had not really appreciated how much home and friends had meant. He'd sort of almost taken them for granted, he thought, with a small degree of shame. Now he'd make it up to all of them!

The Fisherman's Arms was a cosy pub, the bar panelled in dark wood rescued from one of the many shipwrecks the rocky shores of the Bay had claimed over many centuries. It was a good place to be in company, but if you were the last man in, an uneasy atmosphere began to permeate. Maybe a previous landlord had not been so hospitable and was anxious to encourage the last lingering drinkers to finish up and go home... or maybe some of the emotions of fear and panic had been absorbed into the shipwrecked timbers and still lingered there. Whatever it was, no-one seemed keen to remain there alone. Or perhaps Richard had deliberately invented or elaborated on the faint rumours that the place was haunted.

Tales of ghosts and supernatural happenings were not unusual in places where smuggling took place. They were either true and reluctantly admitted to, or they were very effective methods of scaring away nosey-parkers. Whichever, the stories definitely created an atmosphere which remained long after the tellers had gone.

The Fisherman's Arms had been the scene of an exciting episode in Reub's early smuggling days, when a huge cargo of contraband brandy had been piled from the beach into the tunnel below, and Reub and Zack and their mates had been trapped by an over-enthusiastic Revenue man and his team of Dragoons. The kegs of brandy should have been delivered up into the cellar of the pub where the landlord was waiting to receive them, but the smugglers had been intercepted and tied up, the landlord had been cleverly waylaid by a second Revenue officer, and the 'run' had ground to a complete halt.

Reub recalled that was the night that young Matthew had disobeyed Zack's orders to stay at home, but the boy's curiosity had got the better of him. He had followed the smugglers, and from his hiding place where he was watching the activity he had seen the approach of the Revenue man. Bravely running into the tunnel and facing his father's intense displeasure, he was able to alert them to the dangers. He was also the only one small enough to crawl through the gap into the pub cellar above them, ready to haul the kegs up into the store. However, he had got trapped, and spent a frightening night hiding from the Dragoons. From that night on, though, Matt had become one of the smugglers gang himself, and was secretly proud of his new adult status.

Isabella Granger flapped her apron at the rowdy fishermen cluttering up her kitchen, ineffectually re-enforcing her son's request that they should get out and give her a bit of precious time. Reluctantly, but good naturedly, the group of some of the best mates a man could have left Reub to tell his mother that he had a son, and that, best of all, he was going to be married.

Her reaction was as he expected; one of relief and delight. 'Of course, Ah knew Ah had a grandson… tha knaws tha can't keep a secret like that in a place like this. Aye, and a fine lad he is, too. And Damaris, well, lad, tha's lucky that she waited for thee, even though she had tha bairn. She's a reet bonny lass and could 'ave had plenty of young men after 'er, but no, she weren't interested in any but thee. Tha's a very fortunate young man, and Ah hope tha knaws it.'

'That Ah do, Ma. But Damaris is lucky too! Ah'm a fine catch. Jest leuk what a handsome chap Ah've turned intiv! Aye, we'll mek a grand couple!' he grinned.

Isabella cuffed her big son playfully on the side of his head. 'Well then, get thee along ti thi mates, then come back and Ah'll have thee a spot o' supper ready. Jest like in the old days,' she added somewhat wistfully, knowing that from now on Damaris would be the first woman in his life and he would have his own home. She was happy for him, however, as she gave him a push towards the door. 'Go on, now. Ah'll be waitin' for thee, then we can 'ave a reet good old natter.'

When he had closed the door behind him, she turned to the kitchen range and began to prepare a supper for her son, as a sense of relief finally flooded over her. It was time to put five years of worry behind her. From now on life would be good, with her son home, back to the fishing, a wedding to plan, a new home to fettle, and little Ben, her grandson, growing up in a secure and happy family.

Whilst supper was cooking, Isabella sat by her fireside, deep in thought as to how she could help. An idea began to form in her mind… Yes, that is what she would do.

One man that Reuben did not want to see was waiting on the fringe of his friends when he entered the crowded and noisy bar of the Fisherman's Arms, the ancient pub down near the slipway to the beach.

Benjamin Rymer was an arrogant young farmer who had an unfortunate turn for practical jokes which frequently turned in on himself, leaving him embarrassed and shamefaced, a fact which made him all the more arrogant as he tried to cover his failings. They all remembered how he had caused havoc at the wedding of Jane Moorsom and William Barnard, a prank which could have resulted in his killing William. Benjamin, however, had shrugged and laughed it off.

He also had a reputation as a womaniser, and had long had an eye for the attractive Damaris. During Reuben's absence, his persistence had become a nuisance to her, and the more she fended him off, the more attentive he became, hiding round corners and jumping out and grabbing her, so that eventually her father, Zack, attacked him and gave him a good thumping.

That only made matters worse, but now that Reuben was home Ben knew that his chances with Damaris were well and truly over. This knowledge was grudgingly accepted, and resentment simmered, so that when he came face to face with Reuben in the pub, he could not help himself lounging nonchalantly against the bar and saying, 'Well, now. Leuk who's turned up agin. Like the proverbial bad penny. Thowt tha had drownded.'

He shifted his position so that he was closer to Reuben.

'Anyroad, don't be too sure aboot Damaris… she's had plenty o' time ti forget thee. Ah think she fancies me, so watch it.' He grinned round at the men gathered round the bar. 'Tha all knows she's named that bairn of 'ers Ben.' He raised his tankard and took a deep drink. Putting the glass down, and slowly wiping the froth from his upper lip, he paused with careful deliberation, and continued, 'Now why does tha think that might be, eh, Reuben Granger?' He pushed his face close to Reub's, and leered nastily.

Reub could hold his anger back no longer, and with a swift thrust of his bunched fist he landed a cracking blow on Ben's chin, which sent him reeling and his mug of ale flying.

Ben picked himself up, dusted himself down, and wiped his bleeding nose. 'Eh, man! Tha's no need ti take things that serious. Lost tha sense of humour, has tha?'

Still angry, Reub retorted, 'My sense of humour has nivver been better. Only where Damaris is concerned, it becomes a sense of honour. Mek no mistake, Ben's *my* son, and she's goin' ti be *my* wife, so, either say tha's sorry, and leave her alone in future, or else get out. Ah'm here ti celebrate wi' my friends, and at the moment tha's not one of them.'

Ben offered a half-hearted apology with his hand, and reached out to touch Reub. It was not in his nature to back down from a situation. Reuben, however, was not so easily mollified, and turned away, ignoring Ben's gesture.

Ben shrugged and retreated to the other side of the room. His pride had been hurt yet again through his own actions and attitude, but he wasn't going to lose face so much that he had to leave the pub. None of Reub's friends offered to replace the spilt ale, so he bought himself a fresh pint and sat by the fire, moodily eyeing the friendly gathering over the frothy head of the ale.

## 8

Damaris sat by the fire with young Ben on her knee. He'd finished his supper of bread and milk, served in his favourite blue bowl and drizzled with a little honey as a special treat, and had his hands and face scrubbed till they glowed. He hated that, but his mother was ruthless in her cleanliness. Ben had long ago realised it was useless to protest and wriggle, for his mother only scrubbed the harder! It was almost his bedtime, but he was too bewildered by the return of this strange man, and all the excitement it had caused to be ready yet for sleep.

It was cosy sitting like this with his mother. The peat on the fire glowed and gave off a comforting smell of earth and roots and heather. The occasional spark flew up the chimney as the burning peats settled in the grate.

Damaris hugged him to her and rested her chin on his curly head. At last, after five years of uncertainty, she felt contented. Not yet exactly happy - it would take time to erase the sorrows and anxieties of those years - the early days of sudden loss, the subsequent loneliness, then the realisation that she was expecting Reuben's child, the months of discomfort, the fear of the forthcoming birth, and the long years of single parent-hood ahead of her. But now that was all over, and the future looked bright at last.

She knew she had been fortunate in having the love and support of her family. The villagers were a tight-knit community, and families looked after their own. Zack and Liz were as fond of Reub as if he had been their own son, and hoped all along that when he returned he and Damaris would marry. Even if they did not, Liz thought, she and Zack already had a beautiful grandson whom they loved dearly.

It would take some time to re-adjust, Damaris mused, her thoughts winging to the imaginary fire that would burn in the grate of their own cottage - just she, and Reuben, and little Ben with the years of growing up ahead of him. The future would be good, she was quite sure of that. It was time to put the past behind her and look forwards. The events of those years would never be eradicated, either for herself or Reuben - both had experienced far too many emotions for that - but she felt that through fear and hardship, both of them had matured in character.

She hummed quietly, rocking Ben on her knee. Gradually he settled down, drowsy now with the warmth and sounds of the fire, and with the supper of bread and milk softening his hunger. He'd be ravenous again by breakfast time, Damaris smiled. Although he was only small he had an awesome appetite!

He put his thumb in his mouth and started to gently fall asleep. When she could feel his relaxed weight she softly rose from the chair and, with the gentlest of smiles, carried him up the steep and narrow stairs to the traditional box bed built into the alcove beside the chimney breast. That same bed had once been that of her brother Matthew and before him, her uncle of the same name.

Young Matthew now preferred to sleep on a truckle bed up in the attic, further away from the family, and 'uncle' Matthew was long since dead, killed in battle at sea. Young Matthew used to pretend his bed was part of a ship's cabin, and when storms raged outside and battered their cottage walls, sending streams of sea water pouring down their windows, his boyhood dreams were full of swashbuckling adventures.

As she gently laid her son down and smoothed the old patchwork coverlet over him, Damaris' thoughts went back to her own childhood, when her mother had told her stories of the muliticoloured fabrics that made up this now rather shabby family heirloom. There were bits of everyday clothes, memories of special occasions, all woven and stitched into a unique family history.

'It's time,' she thought, 'that I made a new one, one that reflects *my* life, so that I can continue the chapter of the Storm family. I'll ask Jiddy to help me make a start.'

Jiddy was one of Damaris' staunchest friends. She had been part of the life of Baytown folk as long as most of them could remember. No one knew how she had arrived here, a young girl of exotic appearance with her aristocratic Italian parentage. She had been accepted into the community as one of their own - a rare thing in the days when suspicion lurked over every newcomer. Jiddy had subtly become one of the most trustworthy friends a woman - and most of the men - could have. She was strong and athletic, quick of mind, and with a good education behind her, had the wit and knowledge to pick up and memorise snippets of information that became vital to the exploits of the smuggling fraternity into which she was soon accepted.

Many of the women were initially jealous of her beauty and her association with their husbands, but presently came to realise her usefulness, and more important, her loyalty.

Jiddy was also an expert needlewoman earning her living by sewing, mending, and creating new finery for many of the gentry. Her infiltration into the great houses of the district - including those of the leaders of the smuggling syndicates, and even of the chief of the Preventive service - afforded her bits of information that were invaluable to the local smugglers.

Now she came into Damaris' thoughts, not only as a friend, but as an expert dressmaker. Presuming that Reuben would soon formally ask her to marry him, she would need a new dress.

She worried as to how she would afford it. She'd have to have something half decent, although her circumstances did not permit the kind of finery that Jiddy had created for Jane Moorsom - a beautiful gown made from shimmering smuggled silk and trimmed with fine Valenciennes lace.

To try to support the English manufacture of luxury fabrics, the government had banned the import of French fashions. County ladies and the nobility were, however, decidedly snobbish about their finery, and refused to attend public functions unless they were 'suitably' attired. Full-skirted gowns were not the easiest of things to smuggle ashore, though the story went round that a certain duchess managed to secrete over one hundred new gowns in her luggage before she was searched as she came ashore from the French packet boat that plied across the Channel.

Small bales of silk and lace, were, however, much more manageable, and although the gowns themselves were not actually made up in France, experienced local dressmakers were right up to the minute in the fads and fancies of the day, and at least they could still boast that their dresses were the next best thing.

It was ironic that the beautiful Lyons silk worn by Jane, and which would undoubtedly become a family heirloom, had been smuggled in by Reuben. He would not be sneaking in anything so fine for her, she mused with a slight degree of understandable jealousy. No, something much more humble would deck out Damaris, though her love would be none the less, and in Reuben's eyes she would still be the most beautiful girl he knew. She shrugged away her envy, for although Jane had had a fine wedding and married into a good and happy family, she, Damaris, would have Reuben, and... she added, she already had his son, and not for worlds would she change that.

## 9

Midnight was nearly upon them as the friends, with much celebratory shaking of hands and back-slapping in delight at the safe return of Reuben, finally left the warmth of the fire and camaraderie of the Fisherman's Arms after a homecoming celebration that would be remembered for months. Reuben, naturally, had been the centre of attention, bombarded with questions which he fended off good naturedly, saying there were tales to while away many a forthcoming winter evening.

At the moment, however, his own priorities lay with finding out how the community had fared during his absence. He'd worried about further repercussions after his capture and was relieved to learn that no other arrests had taken place, though the smuggling fraternity had kept a very low profile for several months. The few in-coming cargoes of contraband had been landed well out of sight of the village, with Reuben's old friends from the nearby hamlet of Stainsacre, James and Jonas, both experienced and crafty men, taking charge.

Silas grinned and tapped the side of his nose confidentially. 'Aye, there were still the odd nights when Jenny were a'comin', fer we still 'ad ti keep t'squire's hidey-hole topped up. Bye lad, that fella can't 'arf shift 'is brandy!' Silas gave Isaac a wicked wink, and they both guffawed raucously.

Reuben heard that there had been changes in the Preventive force that formerly patrolled the village. Even though smuggling was beginning to be less important, due to the taxes being reduced, thus making the rich profits harder to earn, there was a much greater government presence all along the coast. The old familiar officers, Peter Maxwell, James Herbert, and even fat old Constable

Jos Clarke, with whom they all had many an altercation, had all retired. James and Jos had left the district. Peter Maxwell had recently retired to a farm nearby, and was still seen from time to time in the village, standing by the slipway and looking thoughtfully out to sea.

They had been replaced with a 'reet nosey owd devil' in the form of Horatio Roberts. He'd been sent up from Kent with a whole posse of keen new recruits. They had a base in the old watch-house, and even had their own boat, a small fast cutter, which they had become far too expert in manning and launching.

'Aye, things ain't the same as in t'good owd days.' Even Jos Clarke had been known to take the odd bribe or 'gift' left on his doorstep, usually with a roughly written and threatening note. It was rumoured that it was due to his 'obliging' nature that Jos and his wife had lived so well, and got fat on the proceeds. Reub chuckled at the memory of the very plump Constable puffing up the steep hill in the impatient company of his betrayer, Thomas Duke, on the night he was captured.

'A warnin', Reub. Best give 'Lord Nelson' a wide berth.'

Nobody had seen Ben Rymer slink out after a respectable amount of time had elapsed. They had been so intent on their own news that no one could honestly say that they had missed him. There was something about him that was not right. His practical jokes were often on the dangerous side - maybe that was what sparked his imagination - and made him seek attention. He had no regular girl, but pestered every handsome female in the village. He was part of the farming community, but way back there must have been salt in his blood as he was always trying to worm his way into the close-knit fishing fraternity. There was a feeling of relief in the air once they realised he had left the inn.

A very jovial atmosphere soon emerged, as Reuben had much to tell his mates who all clamoured round him, buying him drinks and persuading him to tell of all his adventures. 'Eh! 'Ang on a bit, lads!' he exclaimed, raising his hand to ward them off. 'Ah've only been 'ome a few hours. Ah've been away fer five years, remember. A lot of tides 'ave ebbed and flowed, aye, and a lot of things 'ave 'appened to me. Far too many to start on jest now. All in good time,' he protested as his friends, having reassured him as to their safety, were not so easily deterred. It was not often that one of their community had had the experiences and, they had to admit - even under Reuben's circumstances - the opportunities to see the world.

Admittedly, several of their fathers had been on the Baltic timber trade runs. A few had even sailed across the Atlantic to America, coming home with tales of other lands. Many of their cottages bore traces of their voyages with souvenirs on the mantelpieces and paintings of their ships upon the walls. A number of cottages even boasted a parrot in a cage. Some of the fathers had been in the navy, but mainly by choice rather than conviction, though some had been caught by the infamous Press Gangs that roamed the dark and narrow streets of Whitby.

The Press Gangs had not much success in Robin Hood's Bay, as the gallant women got wind of their presence as soon as they appeared, beating loud warnings on their saucepans, and the braver ones actually physically attacked the gangs with rolling pins. Meanwhile, the men secreted themselves in cellars or made a run to the densely wooded country through Marner Dale and the aptly named The Bolts.

It was not through cowardice that they escaped or hid themselves, but downright common sense, for if they were captured they were unable to support their families. Making a living was hard enough and the loss of even one man from a boat's crew could mean the difference between survival and starvation. This toughness was inbred for generations in their sons and daughters, along with an intense loyalty to their families and mates.

Reuben finally put up his hands, rose to his feet and told them, 'Reet, that's enough fer tonight. Ah'm away now fer me supper. And that'll be a king's banquet after the stuff Ah've eaten these last months, Ah can tell thee. Be good lads, now, and let me away. Time enough ti tell thee me tales roond this fire for many months yet!' he smiled, as they protested. Reuben's return had sparked off a great deal of excitement amongst his mates.

'Tha'd best all be saving tha brass, 'cos tha'll hev ti buy me a lot of ale, if tha's to hear all me stories. Aye, Ah reckon Ah'll be alreet fer me beer fer quite a while.' He gave a broad wink, and swaggered ostentatiously towards the street door.

'And,' he turned and added, 'give us a break if tha sees me and Dam goin' along t'shore in t'mornin. Ah've gotten summat pretty important ti say tiv 'er. Ah thinks tha might guess what that may be, so,' - tapping the side of his nose with his forefinger, and beaming the happiest smile his friends had seen all evening - 'give us a wide berth, will tha?' With that he rose and went through the stout oak door to the familiar street, pausing a moment to drink in the cool night air of his beloved village, before turning away up the alleyway to his mother's house.

He gave a deep sigh of satisfaction and pure pleasure.

## 10

Next morning he was up early, and away to his workshop in the lean-to shed behind his mother's cottage. Opening the door for the first time in five years, the hinges creaked, and the sun shone through the swirling motes of dust as the draught disturbed them. Cobwebs lay thickly in the window corners, and spiders, resenting the intrusion, scurried to safety. Reub was surprised that Isabella had not been in with her mop and duster, but maybe she could not bear to intrude on the memories.

He stood for a while, looking at the familiar tools and piles of wood, bundles of hazel twigs and balls of netting twine. He'd have to get on making a new fleet of lobster pots, but first, he had something more important to make.

Humming to himself, he rummaged around until he found a chunky piece of pinewood. His tools lay where he had last used them, for he had had no time to come home and leave things as he would have liked. They were dusty and some had rusted where the roof had leaked water onto them.

He picked up a small saw, reached for an oilcan and a rag, and began to clean it up. He gripped the wood firmly in the jaws of the vice, again oiling the screws so that they ceased to squeak at each turn, and happily began to saw the wood to length. Oh yes, he'd soon have the old place licked back into shape. He began to feel very contented.

My, it was good to be back. The old workshop still had its familiar smell of wood and tar and paint, mingled with a faint smell of fish. Reub stretched his arms above his head, and breathed deeply.

Next, he took out the whetstone and sharpened his favourite knife. Well, if he was honest, his *second* favourite knife, for the best one had betrayed his presence in the old church the night he had been captured, and after it had been produced as evidence, he had never seen it again. A pity, for it was a good knife, given by his father, and engraved with his initials. Reub had been so proud of that knife, and had carried it with him everywhere. Oh well, that was all in the past, and this morning he had an important job to do.

He took an old lobster pot to the door-way and, upending it to use as a stool, sat happily in the morning sunshine, whittling a crude but serviceable boat for little Ben. Reub never forgot his promises, and remembering the lad's obvious disappointment of the previous afternoon, determined he would make things right for his son. 'My son!' he mused as he whittled.

This morning, no matter what, young Ben would have priority, even over what he had to say to Damaris. They were a family now, come what may, and he was going to delight in that. Damaris would understand, and probably appreciate Reub's thoughtfulness even more. Reub knew that Damaris was confident and would wait, but his homecoming had obviously been a bit of a puzzlement to the five-year-old child, and he must be won over at the first opportunity.

Reub gave the hull a rough sanding, drilled a hole for the mast, inserted a bit of the hazel he used for making the bow of his lobster pots, and cut a rough sail from his painting cloth. It was somewhat multicoloured but looked cheerful enough from cleaning brushes. He gave the hull a quick coat of thin varnish – Ben could paint it later, whatever colour he chose. Reub would enjoy bringing the boy to the workshop, and letting him choose the paint. They would have some good times together, pottering in the workshop... father, and son. He put the boat outside in the warm sun to dry whilst he began on a bit of tidying up. The disused workshop would soon be put to rights. He'd have to go gathering more hazel for the new lobster pots, as the old bundles may have got too brittle with age, and new twine would be needed for the nets. Ben could go with him and help in gathering the wood. In no time he would be back into the old routines.

Soon he could teach Ben to make his own lobster pot, and imagined how thrilled the boy would be when he caught his first lobster. He recalled his own pride when he had taken his first catch home to his mother, and how good it had tasted when she had cooked it for his tea! Reub was very contented indeed.

Finally, he picked up the finished boat, tied a length of string to the bows, wound it round the hull and stuffed the whole thing in his pocket. Whistling merrily, he closed his workshop door and set off for the Storms' cottage on the other side of the village. It was a lovely morning, and he felt happier than he had for a very long time. It seemed strange having firm ground under his feet once more, and for quite a while he found himself bracing his legs against the movement of a deck that was no longer there. It was an odd sensation.

Slowly he opened the door and called out, 'Anybody at 'ome?'

He was answered by a small whirlwind hurtling down the steep and narrow stairs. Little Ben shot into the room, took a quick look at Reub's empty hands, and stopped in dismay.

'Oh! Ah thowt we was goin' sailin' this mornin',' he said politely, but with an unmistakeable hint of disappointment. 'You said we was,' he added somewhat accusingly.

'Well, now! So we were,' replied Reub, scratching his head. 'Darn it, if Ah didn't completely forget,' he teased, then when he saw the child's eyes cloud with the start of unshed tears, he swept him into his arms and hugged him tight. Holding him away at arms length, he gently wiped the tears with a finger, smiled at the child and said, 'Can tha' do any magic?'

Little Ben shook his head and said 'But Jennet can!'

'Ah! Jennet,' said Reub, remembering the strange step-grandmother of Damaris, the old wise-woman of the village who could produce wonderful herbal cures, was also reputed to be able to cast spells and love potions, and even on occasions change herself into a white hare.

Reub recalled having helped Silas, Sandy and Isaac carry Jennet down on a makeshift hurdle stretcher from her lonely cottage up beyond the cliffs five years ago when she had suffered a stroke on the very day that the *Kent* was captured and young Matthew had fallen from the boat in which he and Reub were out to collect contraband. He also remembered, with some degree of resentment, that old lady's presence on the night of that fateful Hallowe'en when her eccentric behaviour had triggered off the train of events that had led to his capture. But, he mused, that was all water under the bridge now, and he must move on.

'Well, where can we find her?' he asked the child.

'Oh, she's up in her old cottage still,' Ben replied. 'But,' he wailed, 'that's miles away!'

'Well, perhaps if we try very hard, we can do some magic of our own,' comforted Reub. 'Now, close thy eyes, and give me thy hand.' Gently he guided the small fingers to the capacious pockets of his fisherman's canvas smock. 'Can'st tha feel owt?' Reub asked, knowing that the answer would be negative, as he teasingly guided the hand to an empty pocket.

'No, there's nothing there,' wailed Ben, rummaging around to make sure.

'Now, squeeze thy eyes tighter, and let's try again, another pocket. Now can'st tha feel owt?'

'Yes! Yes! Yes! I can!' The child was visibly excited, and jiggled his feet.

'Reet, open thy eyes and tek a leuk!'

Reub choked back his emotions as his small son carefully extracted the roughly carved boat, and saw the expression in the child's face. 'Is it for me?' queried little Ben.

'Of course it is!' replied Reub, 'but it's only a bit rough. Ah can mek thee a much better one, but Ah didn't have much time this mornin'… Ah wanted to coom and see thee - and thi mother. Coom on, let's find her, then we can all go down ti t'sea and see if she'll sail!'

As the three of them, hand in hand, swinging little Ben between them, set off down the steep street and approached the slipway to the beach, a group of fishermen raised their heads from the task of readying the cobles for the afternoon tide. They waved to Reub, touched their caps to Damaris, and with a wink and a friendly nod, deliberately resumed their work. They were all happy for the lass, almost as if she was their own daughter.

It was a beautiful early autumn morning, with the summer's warmth yet in the air, and with the still clarity that only comes on rare mornings in the spring and the autumn. The gentle tide was well out, and the clear blue of the sky reflected white clouds on the surface of the water. The beach was firm and clean, and walking south towards Mill Beck, the world appeared as near perfect to the young couple.

Ben broke away and ran excitedly towards a large rock pool with water deep enough to launch his boat. After careful inspection, he came running back to Reub and tugged his gansey. 'Ah've found a reet good place for t'boat, Reub! Coom on, let's get her launched!'

Reub turned to Damaris with a grin, and inclined his head towards the excited child. 'All reet, lad, Ah'm comin!' and hand in hand they set off over the scaurs to the favoured pool. Damaris held back, brushing the hair from her eyes, at the same time, dashing away the tears of happiness that welled there, watching her son and his father sharing at last that special bond. She had the wisdom to retreat to a distant rock and sat watching them on their own, beginning to forge a new relationship, one that she hoped would last for a very long time.

From time to time the two absorbed sailors turned and gave her a wave, and eventually, Reub said something to Ben, who nodded and began to load his boat with small pebbles and shells. Reub straightened up and slowly walked over to where Damaris was sitting. Carefully he sat beside her and put his arms round her shoulder. Still keeping a watchful eye on the small boy happily playing with his boat, Reub turned to her and raised her head for the gentlest of kisses. Damaris snuggled into his neck and sighed with a great happiness. 'Ah thowt Ah'd nivver see this day,' she said.

'There'll be lots more like this, and better,' replied Reub. 'Wait until there's two - or three - little lads playin' wi' boats!' he teased her. Before she could remonstrate, he took her hand and slid on to one knee on the sand, and there, under the perfect autumn sky, with a calm sea beyond, and his son playing in the rock pool, Reuben finally formally proposed to Damaris, and with an unspeakable joy, she accepted.

## 11

They sat close together on the warm rock in a companionable silence. The incoming tide murmured gently on the sand, where the small waves curled and broke, running forward and pouring themselves into the rockpools. A flock of opportunist small brown and white plovers chased the waves, seeking the tiny crustacea the sea was bringing for their sustenance. They were joined by a dozen or so more stately oyster-catchers, the smartest birds on the shore, with their immaculate black and white plumage and scarlet legs and beaks. As each small wave receded until the next one took its place, the birds followed, probing deep, their reflections mirrored in the wet sand. They made a beautiful sight, and the young couple sat, leaning their shoulders together and watched in peaceful stillness.

No words needed to be spoken, but after a while Damaris broke the silence and confessed, 'The day Ah really first accepted that Ah'd marry thee was the day tha made me that ring from grass. Ah still have it, tha knows. The way tha wove those two strands of grass together, Ah thowt, that's how Reub and I should be, woven together into a perfect circle.' Reub was thoughtful, touched by her sensitive philosophy, and determined to have a special wedding ring made from two strands of gold in the same design, that would symbolise their complete togetherness.

He choked back the lump in his throat and turned away to look at his son, happily playing with his boat. He was relieved to discover that the past five hard years among tough and often callous men had not eliminated his romantic streak.

Reub was still not accustomed to the daily presence of a five-year-old child, one who he had not even known had existed. He found he was regretting missing the precious years of his son's babyhood - his first stumbling steps, his first attempts at speech, feeling his first teeth… 'Not to mention all the sleepless nights,' added Damaris. 'And all the extra washing!'

Hiding his embarrassment, he took Damaris by the hand, and still focussing on young Ben, he shouted, 'Oy! Ben! Coom along now… dinner time!'

Realising he was hungry, the boy picked up his boat, carefully unloaded his cargo of pebbles and shells, shook off the drops of salt water, and happily trotted over to his parents. They were standing close together hand in hand. He could not part them, so after a moment's consideration, he moved round and slipped his small wet hand into Reub's, looked up with a cheeky grin and said, 'That boat's alreet, but Ah could get more stuff in a bigger one!'

Reub gave him a playful cuff on the shoulder, and together the new family moved off the shore. They suspected that in spite of Reuben's pleas for privacy, they had surreptitiously been watched and that speculation would be rife. As they approached the slipway they knew they had been right, for they were to be greeted with whoops and cheers from the waiting fishermen, who, in spite of their promise to give the young couple some space, knew perfectly well what had been going on.

A chorus of cheeky wolf-whistles made them laugh with embarrassment. Shouts of 'When's t'weddin', then?'

'Can we all come?'

'Bye, lad, that's grand news, so it is!'

'Glad ti see he's mekkin an 'onest woman of thee, Dam!'

'Are t' sure tha wants ti marry 'im, cos Ah'm still available!'

From the wide grins on everyone's faces it was evident that all except one watcher were happy for them.

Ben Rymer slouched away un-noticed.

## 12

After dinner, Reub followed Zack down into the cellar where he kept and worked on his lines and nets, and often also hid incoming contraband until it could be moved on. It was a risky business, as they all well knew, but in hard times being involved with smuggling was the only way a family could survive financially.

In winter, when the seas pounded relentlessly against the cliffs, the fishing boats could be laid up for days or even weeks, and with no income likely, things could, and did, get desperate. To become involved with the local smuggling gang would ensure good money, with a single night's involvement in handling the profitable contraband bringing in as much cash as a whole week's fishing. As they all knew to their cost, however, this involvement was not undertaken lightly, and secrecy and discretion were paramount.

Like most of the other fishing cellars in the village, Zack's held a number of well-concealed hiding places. False ceilings, hollow beams, loose stones in the walls, gaps under the floorboards, and provision for speedily creating a hole in the wall for contraband to be quickly passed through to next door. A network of tunnels and passageways known only to those concerned enabled the swift movement of goods, and the Revenue officers were often unaware of what was happening sometimes beneath their very feet.

The Storms knew this routine only too well, as their involvement had gone back several generations. Zack's parents, Isaac and Rebecca, now well into their nineties, but still sharp in mind if not so nimble in body, currently delighted in telling their adventures to young Ben, just as they had to Damaris and Matthew in their young days. Time had moved on, but circumstances had barely changed; life was not much easier now than it was then.

Zack was showing signs of age, and Reub noticed with a pang of sorrow, how the once dark hair and beard were grizzled with grey, and the once straight back was painfully bent with the rheumatism which affected most of the ageing fishing community, due to long hours working in cold and wet conditions.

The elderly fisherman spent a lot of time down here, supposedly messing about with his fishing gear, but often just coming down to think about the future. He liked his own space, and time apart from Liz and the family. None of them ever came down here uninvited. It was Zack's domain and respected as such.

It was dark down there, with no windows onto the outside world, and that gave the cellar a sense of secrecy and security. Zack carefully closed the trapdoor through which they had entered, reached for a lantern and his tinderbox, and once there was a faint glow emanating from the candle, Zack carefully sat himself down on an upturned lobsterpot and gestured that Reub should do the same. Taking out his pipe, he slowly filled and lit it, looking enquiringly over the smouldering bowl and offering it over to Reub to take a draw. Reub shook his head and regarded the older man with guilt and sorrow. It was surely largely due to his carelessness in being captured and sent away that the Storm family were in this situation. Reub should have been shouldering the harder part of their fishing partnership, instead of leaving it to Zack.

Matt had resentfully taken his place, but there was not the filial affection and bond that there should have been, as Matt still harboured his long-held ambition to train as an officer and go to sea in the navy. The feeling of resentment was still strong, and to keep things as peaceful as possible, Zack had shouldered the bulk of the work. He would have not have minded so much if Matt had used his spare time to study instead of loafing about, idly harbouring his grudge.

'Well, now, Zack. What are we goin' ti deah aboot all this? Ah've bin thinkin' and worryin' and what Ah suggest is that Ah coom back inti partnership wi' thee, and then we can let Matt go his own way. Give t'lad a fair chance, like. Ah've learned a lot aboot seamanship while Ah was away, and there's nowt like practical experience. Tha can't learn everything from books. If young Matt will stop bein' so damned surly, Ah know Ah can help 'im a lot. In fact, Ah thowt aboot 'im all t'time Ah was away, and Ah did 'ave a word wi' Captain Searle aboot 'im.

'Funny, that,' mused Reub, 'that it should 'ave been owd Searle what rescued Matt when we was shot oot o' the coble by Stoney Fagg, that last battle wi' t'*Kent*! Searle remembered t'lad, and how he was that tekken wi' the grand cabin, and said that was where he wanted ti end up! He were that amazed when Ah towd him that Ah hoped ti marry the lad's sister.'

Reub fiddled with a length of fishing net, examining it carefully before adding, 'Ah think Ah'm not boasting if Ah tell thee that Cap'n Searle had a bit of a soft spot for me. Once Ah'd got over me 'omesickness, Ah really enjoyed life on that ship, and Ah did some things that must 'ave gained the owd man's respect.' Zack looked up enquiringly, but Reub shook his head and smiled. 'Nay, Ah'm not tellin' thee, 'cos tha'd go and spout to Damaris, and then where would Ah be! Some things she'd best not know,' he said, reflectively.

'Anyroad,' continued Reuben, 'Ah towd 'im aboot young Matt wanting ti be an officer, and that 'cos Ah'd ended up there fer five years, that seemed to have put paid ti t'lad's future. Searle asked if Matt was really as bright and loyal as he appeared at that short interview, and Ah said, yes 'e was, though 'e was a mite surly. No more was said, until Searle was alongside t'purser who paid me me last wages. Granger, he said, remember that young friend o' yourn what wants ti go in t'navy? Give 'im a helping 'and, get 'im studyin' - there's a chance if 'e works 'ard and passes 'is exams, Ah might jest find 'im a place aboard as a midshipman. Then owd Searle give me one o' his rare smiles - if tha can call it a smile - and wishes me luck and tells me not to forget what 'e just said. He'd be a good Captain to work under, strict but fair.'

'Trouble is,' confided Reub, 'tha saw Matt's attitude when Ah came back. 'E won't like tekkin advice and edication from me while 'e's in this mood.'

Zack removed his pipe and scratched his head thoughtfully. 'Ah'll 'ave a word wi grandad Isaac. 'E gave Matt 'is navigation books, and fer a tahme before tha went away, nowt would get 'is 'ead oot o' them, even though 'e didn't really understand all t'mathematics and sich. Ah couldn't 'elp 'im much, though me faither did a bit.

'Thing is now, Isaac's eyesight ain't that good, and 'e can't see all t'figures clearly. Ah reckon if Ah have a word wi faither, and we set it up that he sends fer Matt to read for 'im, Matt don't really understand what e's readin', then, all of a surprise, you turn up, tactfully ask ti 'ave a look, and mek it all seem clear and easy, mebbe we'll win 'im over, and no tempers lost! Ow aboot that?'

It would not be an easy job to wean Matt from his accustomed surliness without him losing face. If he really *was* serious about entering the navy, then they would have to watch for the crack opening in his defensive attitude and make their move.

Maybe this was the way. It was certainly worth a try.

'Tha knaws, Zack Storm, tha's a crafty owd bugger! Reet, let's give it a go. T'lad deserves summat better than this.'

## 13

Jiddy Vardy with her dressmaking skills was, naturally, the friend to whom Damaris turned regarding her bridal dress.

The ceremony was to be a quiet one, with just family and friends, unlike the wedding of her friend Jane some six years previously, which was still talked of in the village. Jane, although the daughter of a poor fisherman's widow, had married into a very wealthy farming family, one whose hospitality was legendary and who, loving Jane deeply, had happily taken on all the expense and responsibility of the occasion.

Jane and William's marriage had taken place in the small church which stood on the hill overlooking the village. It had served the community for centuries. A sense of timelessness filled its quiet walls, and a feeling of deep calm pervaded the atmosphere. Even the graveyard with its long grass and weathered tombstones was a place of peace, especially on long summer days when the tall grasses whispered gently in the cooling breeze.

Many of the villagers had ancestors buried here - but those whose loved ones had been drowned at sea and had no such peaceful resting place were deprived of the comfort of bringing flowers, and sitting for a while, communing in their thoughts with those who were so near them yet so far away in body.

The wide-open view swept across the green meadows, the fields golden with corn, to the distant purple moorland and down to the shimmering blue sea. It was a place of great beauty as well as tranquillity.

It had been a wonderfully sunny day, and after the wedding ceremony Jane and William had been carried to the reception in the newly painted farm cart with its shiny yellow wheels. Garlanded with flowers and greenery and colourful ribbons it was drawn by the beautiful white carthorse, Rosie, herself beribboned, groomed until her fetlocks resembled a fluff of white feathers, her hooves oiled and polished to a mahogany gleam for the occasion. It was difficult to know who held their head the proudest as they pulled away from the church followed by crowds of well-wishing friends - Jane or Rosie!

Reub and his friends, still caught up in the regular smuggling runs, had sneaked in a bale of fine Lyons silk and several yards of delicate Valenciennes lace from which Jiddy had created a magnificent wedding dress, one which was the envy of many of the county ladies and which had been the cause of Jiddy's order book being full for months.

There would be no such dress and elaborate ceremony celebrated with a huge and generous feast for Damaris, as she was already a mother. The family had struggled financially without Reub's partnership in the boat, and with Zack's reluctance to take as full a part in the incoming smuggling runs following Reub's capture. For several months after, the entire smuggling community was keeping a low profile and money was still tight, with little left over except for the provision of absolute necessities.

However, Jiddy was determined not to let the occasion pass without something special for two of her dearest friends' big event. She already had a few ideas in mind when she called on Damaris and Liz to talk it over. Damaris had taken to wearing the drab skirts and shawls common to most of the fisherwomen in the village, but Jiddy recalled her wearing a pretty blue wool dress, exactly the colour of her eyes, when she was a young girl.

'Reet, then. Let's see what we can find for thee.' Jiddy took charge of the situation in her indomitable manner. Many would have called her downright bossy, but Liz and Damaris knew her well enough to realise that she meant well. They managed a secret smile to each other as Jiddy elbowed them out of her way and began rummaging through the pile of clothes in the old cedar dower chest. In no time at all Jiddy emerged slightly dishevelled but triumphant with the old blue dress.

'There!' she exclaimed, pulling the shawl from Damaris' head and unpinning the long blonde hair from its tight bun, and holding the dress up. 'It's perfect!'

'But, Jiddy! Ah can't get inti that! Leuk how much bigger Ah've got since Ah had Ben! Mebbe t'length's not bad, but leuk at the waist!'

'Hum,' said Jiddy, holding her head on one side with a teasing expression in her dark eyes. 'Now, why didn't I think of that? Never mind...' and she dived into her sewing kit and produced a large pair of scissors, and before Damaris could protest, for Jiddy always worked so quickly, her actions were like a whirlwind, she expertly sliced the dress from hem to neck and spread it open on the bed. Damaris recoiled in horror.

'Jiddy! What has tha done. Tha's ruined it, and it was ma best dress even though Ah cannot wear it ony more,' and the tears welled in her eyes. Jiddy threw her arms around the distressed young woman, and simply said, 'Trust me.' Bundling up the ruined garment, she thrust it into her bag, and remarked with a knowing sideways look and an irrepressible twinkle in her sloe-dark eyes, 'Well, I'll have to repair that now, won't I?'

Some days later she returned, and opened a neatly packed parcel. Inside lay the blue dress, but what a transformation. The fine wool had been cleaned and pressed, and inserted was a beautiful panel of blue and cream striped silk. The waist had been reshaped and trimmed with a discreet bow of blue ribbon, and the bodice, widened to take Damaris' full figure, was filled with a panel of the same striped silk, laced across with fine blue ribbons. A simple white lace cap, again trimmed with blue, completed the outfit.

Damaris was speechless, and Liz turned to Jiddy with a great glow of gratitude in her tired eyes, and said, 'Jiddy, my dearest friend, how can we ever thank you. I had worried so much about sending Damaris to her wedding in something fitting. I might have known that you would work your usual magic. Put it on, Dam, and let's have a proper look. Pass that hairbrush... '

Removing her workaday clothes, Damaris slipped the altered gown over her head and Jiddy smoothed it expertly over her hips. It fitted perfectly, even though Jiddy had taken the barest of measurements. She smiled, and pointed to her eyes - 'I trust these, you see!'

Damaris looked in the ancient speckled mirror. The reflection that looked back at her, although not quite that of the young girl of her carefree youth, was certainly that of a very beautiful woman.

She was speechless, but Jiddy did not need words of thanks. All she needed was to see the expression in those clear blue eyes. 'There you are!' she said, to diffuse the emotion of the moment. 'I said you could trust me, didn't I? And,' she added, putting her finger to her lips, 'don't ask me where that silk came from, because it's best that you don't know!'

# - 14 -

Isaac and Rebecca Storm, Zack's parents, still lived in the same cottage in The Bolts, where their tiny garden bordered the King's Beck which flowed down from the high moorland on its way to the open sea. On warm, fine days, Isaac would happily potter in his shed, tending plants to brighten the house, which cheered Rebecca who could only manage to walk as far as the front door, where she sat in the sun and kept an eye on Isaac. By her side stood a large brass bell, with which she could summon him if needed. Sometimes he fell asleep in the shed, and the ringing of Rebecca's bell jolted him out of his slumbers. He never admitted to nodding off - explaining to Rebecca that he couldn't always immediately drop what he was doing.

The bell rang, and Isaac ignored it. It rang again, urgently, so he left his plants and went back to the cottage. 'Tha's nivver learnt patience, woman. What does tha want now?' Isaac saw the excited twinkle in her eye before he shielded his eyes against the sun and saw the familiar figure of Reuben striding down the alleyway. Determined to tease her, he exclaimed, 'Who's that comin' along t'path. Dean't want ony strangers nosin' around 'ere. Ah'll gang along and send 'im off.'

'Nay, Isaac! 'Tis Reuben come back!'

'Nivver in this world. Dean't want no strangers...' he muttered, and with that he picked up his spade and tottered off down the path. He knew all along that it was Reuben, and gave the returning man a big grin and a sly wink, before pretending to strike him with the spade. Rebecca was beside herself, frustrated that she couldn't get to the two men down the alleyway, and terrified when she saw Isaac raise his spade. Reaching down, she grabbed the bell and rang it for all she was worth. Isaac turned round, and Reuben waved as he took the spade from the old man, and flung his arms round the frail shoulders. 'What on earth art tha playin' at, Isaac? Tha knew it was me, surely... oh, tha's not still teasing Rebecca?' he queried, and shook his finger in front of Isaac. 'Tha's a wicked owd man, dost tha know that? Poor owd leddy, 'tis a wonder she han't got rid o' thee years agone.'

Isaac chuckled and winked broadly. 'Nay,' he said, 'she'll hev ti put up wi' me a bit longer.'

Reuben guided the old man, grinning broadly, to the doorway where Rebecca was struggling to rise from her chair to greet him. 'Oh, Reub, Ah nivver thowt Ah'd live ti see this day. Let's 'ave a leuk at thee! My, tha's a handsome chap! If Ah were a few years younger, no young lass would have a chance with thee! Coom away in. Isaac!' she called, 'put t'kettle on, and get the new bread and fix some toast. Butter's in t'larder - plenty of it, now, we're celebratin'. Dean't put fork too close ti t'fire, and put plenty o' tea inti t'pot!'

'Aye, aye, alreet. Bossy owd besom, Ah knows how ti mek tea and toast, Ah've had plenty o' practice,' he muttered as he set about his given tasks. Reuben gave him a conspiratorial wink, and settled down beside Rebecca, taking her gnarled and arthritic hand gently in his.

'It's reet good ti be 'ome agin, Rebecca. Ah wanted ti coom and see thee both before onybody else towd thee the news. Damaris has agreed ti be me wife, and Ah'm that chuffed Ah could shout and sing,' he admitted with a shamefaced smile. 'And as for young Ben, why, ain't he a cracker!'

Rebecca gently squeezed Reub's rough, calloused hand in congratulation. Little Ben had become a great delight to them both, and brought back so many memories of happier times. Perhaps now the family could start to get back on an even keel.

Reub watched with a smile of amusement as Isaac opened the beautiful mahogany tea-caddy which he so well remembered keeping full to the brim, along with the tobacco jar which still stood on the mantelpiece. The old man generously scooped the fine black leaves into the waiting ready-warmed teapot. His hands were not as steady as they used to be, Reub observed, and a few leaves scattered onto the white tablecloth. Rebecca tutted in annoyance. She still liked everything to be just so. 'Fussy old besom,' Isaac muttered again.

He tottered over to the fire and reached for the thick woollen kettle holder which hung on a hook by the fireside. 'Here, let me do that,' said Reub, putting a hand on the old man's.

'Aye, thank'ee, Reub. Ah'm not as steady as Ah was, but we manage. Mind, tha might 'ave saved me anither tellin' off if Ah'd spilt t'watter on t'floor!'

'Anyroad, Ah see tha still manages ti get plenty o' tea!' remarked Reub with a grin, remembering how he had so enjoyed keeping this lovely old couple well supplied with the little luxuries of their lives during his smuggling days. Old Isaac and also Rebecca had done their bit in trading contraband in their young - and not so young - days, and they had delighted sharing the reminiscences of their adventures with a young Damaris and Matthew, and now looked forward to the days when Ben would also be old enough to hear the tales himself.

'Oh aye, we're well set up,' commented Rebecca, 'but there was a time when even *our* supply of tea was scarce.' She reached out for a slice of toast and spread it thickly with the rich country butter. She took a bite, savoured the taste, and followed it with a hearty sup of tea. Mopping her lips delicately with the pure white napkin she had tucked under her chin, for even at her great age Rebecca was fastidious, she put down the cup and began her tale.

Soon after Reuben's arrest, the main Preventive Officer in Baytown, Peter Maxwell, had decided to take an early retirement. He and his partner James Herbert had been stationed in the area longer than most, as usually the Preventive men, especially the dishonest ones, were moved on after a relatively short spell of duty. Because of low wages many became familiar with the local smuggling fraternity, taking heavy bribes to turn a blind eye and a deaf ear. Maybe Peter and James had been both honest and efficient, so the Government had left them in place. An odd sort of respect had grown between these two officers and the community in which they worked, which, all things considered, must have been somewhat unusual.

Rebecca was certain that Peter had suspected that she had been in possession of a large keg of brandy one night when he was detailed to search her house, after a large consignment of contraband had been intercepted. His search had been courteous and not too thorough. A beam from his lantern had caught the edge of what appeared to be a barrel-shaped and uncomfortable stool on which she had been sitting, somewhat breathless. Isaac was nowhere to be seen, so, smiling to himself, Peter had left the old lady in peace.

Rebecca told how Peter was still in the area, but had left Government employment and bought a small farm up on the nearby moorland. He came down into the village occasionally to his favourite pub, but apart from that he was rarely seen.

Things had changed when his replacement arrived, however. Horatio Roberts had descended on the village with a keen sense of duty. He would sort this place out, once and for all! Landings had to be delayed, and contraband already hidden in the village would have to stay out of sight for a while, until the smugglers got his measure and found a weak spot in his armour. He was the worst kind of 'sniv', with an uncanny knack of sniffing things out.

Word rapidly spread round the village, and there was a sudden spurt of activity in 'household repairs' as loosened floorboards were lifted, small kegs and boxes and packages secreted underneath and the boards nailed firmly back down. Loose stones in walls were removed, the cavities behind hollowed out, then firmly mortared back in place, hiding their secrets from prying eyes. Trapdoors into cellars were craftily hidden under heavy pieces of furniture, and hanging ropes in chimneys relieved of their burdens, and neatly coiled out of sight. Contraband had gone 'under cover', and maybe some of it was never recovered, but remained behind walls and under floorboards for ever more. Who knows?

Rebecca stopped digressing and got on with her story. 'Tha remembers William and Mary Cobb, doesn't tha?' she asked. Reuben nodded, his mouth full of the delicious toast. William was one of the village's most prosperous grocers. However, he had an unfortunate tendency to be careless where his 'stock' was concerned. Horatio Roberts decided to pay him a courtesy call the day after it had been rumoured that a landing of contraband had taken place. Entering the shop, Roberts went through into the back quarters where William and Mary lived.

Unfortunately they had not been quick enough to get the new stock out of sight, for there in the room, in open cupboards, and even laid on the beds, were dozens of packages of tea! William brazened it out, but Mary cowered in the corner, guiltily.

'Do you know about all this, Mrs. Cobb?' Roberts had asked brusquely, peering closely into the terrified Mary's eyes. Mary hid her face in her hands and nodded. 'You realise that all this will have to go?' demanded the delighted Officer.

As Mary stepped back, her heel caught the edge of the bedcover which had been carefully drawn down to the floor. Horatio Roberts' quick eye spotted something else. With a satisfied grin he lifted the cover, and drew out three small kegs of best Hollands gin. 'Is this yours?' he enquired. Mary nodded then shook her head in total confusion. She was supposed to be a staunch follower of the famous Methodist leader John Wesley who regularly preached in the newly converted small chapel right next door! 'Naughty! Very naughty!' smirked Roberts, as he dragged the kegs from under the bed. 'What would the good Mr. Wesley have to say about all this, then? He doesn't hold with strong drink, does he, Mrs. Cobb?'

So, continued Rebecca, the tea and the gin were confiscated and William Cobb's customers had a long period without their favourite beverage.

During tea, the subject of Matthew naturally arose, and Reub confided to Isaac Zack's plan for breaking the ice over the navigation studies. Together they hatched a plan, that Isaac would send for Matt the very next evening, and Reub would call by as if by chance, and they would see how things went. Reub wondered if it was too soon after his return, but Isaac was all for setting things straight as soon as possible.

The family were sitting down to supper when a message came for Matthew. His grandfather had apparently discovered some old family papers which he needed help in reading, as the handwriting was too small for him to see clearly. Although he was tired after a hard day's fishing, Matt had always had time for his grandfather. Isaac was one of the few members of the family he respected and admired, and so it was that he made his way along The Bolts on the evening that would change his life.

'Noo then, grandad. What's all this aboot? Let's 'ave a leuk. Why!' he exclaimed, 'this is all aboot who built this house over a hundred years since! It's been in t'Storm fambly all that tahm.'

'Aye, and it'll continue that way, Matt, for Rebecca and Ah've decided that when we've gone it'll be thine. We hope tha'll get wed, and bring new sons intiv t'owd spot. Keep t'Storms goin', like.'

Matt was touched by the old couple's generosity. 'But,' he said, putting his arms round the old man's frail shoulders, 'that won't be for a long time yet! Ah can't get wed until Ah've gotten some money, an' Ah can't see that comin' from t'fishing, t'way things are these days. We aren't gettin' so much from t'smugglin' like a few years back. Besides,' he blushed, 'Ah dean't 'ave a special girl. There's plenty o' pretty wenches in t'village, but none as who Ah fancy enough ti spend t'rest o' me life wi'. Grandma must 'ave been reet special for tha to have stuck wi' each other this long.' He gave one of his very rare smiles at the old lady sitting by the fire.

'Ah knaw things is 'ard, lad, but noo that Reuben's back and can gang in t'boat with thi faither, there's no reason why tha shouldn't start studying agin. Here, leuk, Ah found some more o' me owd navigation books.' Isaac rummaged under the parchment documents and opened a thick book.

Matt sat down and opened the pages eagerly. Then his face fell. 'But grandad, Ah'll nivver understand all this! It's all figures and sums. Ah can't do it!' He shut the book with a disappointed slam, and slouched back in his chair. Isaac raised his eyes to Rebecca and sighed. He wished Reuben would hurry up.

As if his wish had been granted, the door opened and in breezed Reuben. Matt was still feeling moody, and rose to leave. 'If tha's stoppin' then Ah'm goin,' he muttered.

'Why, what's t'problem?' queried Reub, though he knew perfectly well. 'Hey, Isaac, what's this?' Reub reached for the thick book carefully sewn into its sailcloth cover. 'What course do you set to reach this given landfall... why, that's easy! Tha reads off traverse board ti get the last fix, then tha measures t'strength of t'wind and speed of t'ship by reading t'log line and...' Matthew tried not to look interested or impressed. 'If tha wants, Ah can show thee a few tips, Matt, and mebbe we can get thee away to sea after all. Ah can tell thee a lot o' things that ain't in t'books, a lot o' practical things, like tyin' all the knots tha needs ti knaw in handlin' riggin' and sich. A sailin' ship's a bit different from a coble, tha knaws! Ah owes thee one, lad, and Ah'd like ti help thee... if tha'll let me.'

Rebecca reached for the teapot and with shaking hands poured herself another cup. She looked at it for a long time, her memory reaching back into the past. Aye, things had certainly been hard in the days when she and Isaac had first married, and things were hard again now. If Matthew had any sense and could bury his resentment towards Reuben, he would take this opportunity with both hands. It would mean discipline and hard work, but, my word, that lad would look reet handsome in uniform.

Rebecca sipped her tea and smiled at her grandson. Amazingly, she got a glimmer of a smile in response. Things were certainly looking up

## 15

Captain Joseph Emerson lived in the imposing stone-built house on Fisherhead which had once been occupied by the village Constable, Jos Clarke and his snooty wife Arabella. Whilst Reuben had been away at sea, the time came for Jos to retire and return to his old home town down south. He was, in a way, sorry to go, because he had had a good living here. He'd got the measure of the local population, and had, whether or not his wife had been fully aware of the situation, feathered his nest nicely with the bribes that landed from time to time on his doorstep. He was getting too old and fat for the job, and was happy enough to turn the occasional blind eye to the goings-on of the smuggling community. All he had needed to do was to keep headquarters, fortunately far enough away, informed with regular reports, some of which were not too economical with the truth. He was not alone in this deception, for it was a recognised fact that many of his colleagues did the same, as it was often the only way they could supplement their poorly and irregularly paid wages. Like the smugglers against whom he was supposed to be working, he had to make ends meet one way or another.

Arabella, on the other hand, could not wait to get away. Being the wife of the Constable, she was in a social class of her own, and had no close friends. She was a lonely woman, but would not admit it.

Groups of women fell silent when she approached, and if she went into any of the village shops the sudden silence could be cut with a knife, unless it was advantageous to deliberately let her hear a bit of significant gossip. She always seemed to be around when the fishing boats were coming home, and her sharp eyes and nose had an uncanny knack of sniffing out any contraband hidden under the nets. Many an uneasy fisherman had watched her back as she hastily turned up the steps that led to her home. She would not be much missed.

Captain Emerson had also retired, and was enjoying living in his nice house. He was a widower, but had got used to being on his own and had a daughter living near by who kept an eye on him, cooked his meals and kept him and his house tidy.

On fine warm days he could be found down by the slipway, sitting on a bench overlooking the water and watching the boats or talking of his days before the mast to the eager young boys whose aim was also to go to sea. Captain Emerson never tired of sharing his experiences, and became a well-known and respected figure. If anyone else was sitting on his place on the bench, it was an unspoken rule that they would get up, politely doff their cap to the Captain, and move up to give him his own space. He was very happy down there by the sea, but exasperated his daughter who had frequently to come and find him before his dinner got cold.

On cooler days he kept an eye on things from the window in his attic, where he had installed a powerful telescope.

He had had a successful and profitable career as a Master Mariner and had sailed to many parts of the world. Now in his late eighties, he was an imposing figure with a long white bushy beard, piercing blue eyes, and a remarkably straight back. He was one of the most respected members of the community, and even the mischievous young fisherlads doffed their caps when they met him.

He was, therefore, the ideal person to take young Matt in hand, and give him some lessons in navigation. Quite a few of the old retired sea-dogs had set up informal navigation schools in the village and were passing on their valuable first-hand knowledge and experience to the new generation.

Reuben, therefore, found himself diffidently knocking at Captain Emerson's door with his proposal for Matthew. Reub was understandably uneasy standing there on the doorstep, for this was the very house in which the Constable who had arrested him had formerly lived. As the Captain opened the door, Reuben could see behind him into the imposing hallway with its loudly ticking clock, the hallway in which his informant Thomas Duke had stood on that fateful evening long ago, impatiently waiting until the Constable got himself dressed and was finally ready to accompany Thomas on his journey of betrayal.

Reub removed his woollen cap, and stood there twisting it in his hands. He was not normally nervous of speaking to the Captain, but his presence in this house un-nerved him. Jos Clarke had lived here for as long as Reub could remember, and he almost expected to see his plump figure coming down the stairs.

'Well now, Granger, what can I do for thee?' asked the white bearded Captain.

'It's about young Matt Storm,' replied Reuben.

'Best come inside then, and we'll see what we can do.'

Reuben followed the Captain down the long hall and into the small sitting room that overlooked his tiny garden. It was beautifully tended, and masses of late blooming red roses tumbled over the brick walls of his outhouse. A wicker chair stood in the middle of the tiny patch of grass. On the seat was a battered straw hat. The Captain had obviously been enjoying the late autumn sunshine. Reub observed the evidence of a relaxed retirement, and apologised for disturbing him.

Captain Emerson narrowed his eyes and gave Reub a twinkling smile, indicating a small chair standing by the table. 'Fetch that outside, lad, and let's enjoy this sunshine.'

So there, in the garden of Jos Clarke's former residence, Reuben told the Captain all his worries. The old man listened patiently, nodding his head from time to time, as Reub explained what a difficult youth Matthew had become. Captain Emerson knew all about such attitudes, as he had dealt with many such over the years. He reassured Reuben that he would soon sort him out, and let him gain some self-respect.

'Ah shan't let thee do all this fer nowt,' Reub told the Captain. 'Ah needs to deah mi best fer t'lad, not only because he's mi wife's brother, but it was my fault Ah got captured, and Matt had ti put his own plans aside and help his faither. He was that keen ti get away from t'fishin' once he had seen the inside o'that fine cabin on t'*Pelican*, and Ah can't blame him!' Reub smiled. 'Matt's a bright lad, and if tha can knock some sense intiv 'im, and get his enthusiasm back, Ah knaws he'll not let thee down.'

'Aye, he's a good lad is young Matthew. I'll do my best for him,' said Captain Emerson. 'Now, don't worry about payment. I've nothing to do with my time these days, and it would be grand to have a promising young lad to pass my experience on to. I've no son of my own...' he looked sadly into the distance with his clear blue eyes. 'It will be a great pleasure to me, as long as he works hard, and I'll make sure he does,' twinkled the old man.

Reub got up from the chair, and shook the Captain's hand. Matthew was to start his new studies that very week - so long as he would accept the generous offer of help. Reub shrugged his shoulders.

He would have to wait and see.

## 16

Damaris and Reuben were married after the Sunday morning service in the Wesleyan chapel which overlooked the sea. It was a simple ceremony, with a few favourite hymns and Bible readings. They neither wanted nor could afford a big 'do', and were attended only by their immediate family.

The exceptions were Damaris' best friend Annie Harrison, now happily married to her childhood sweetheart, Richard Bedlington, and the proud mother of two delightful small daughters, and of course, Jiddy Vardy. Reub felt he had never seen Damaris look more beautiful.

Since his return, the lines of anxious worry had left her face, and she had regained the happy and carefree expression of her youth. He was astonished at the transformation of the old blue wool dress, in which he had pictured her in his mind all the time he was away. The colour suited her to perfection, and now with Jiddy's skilful alterations, it was perfect. He was so pleased that she wore the dress of his fond memories for her wedding. Round her neck she wore the jet and silver pendant he had bought her, which he had sent round in its box earlier that morning.

Reuben also looked smart and handsome. Isabella had knitted him a new gansey, a special garment known as a bridal shirt. It still carried the Granger family pattern, but instead of the hard-wearing greys or navy-blues of the working gansey, the bridal shirt was knitted in white. It would be worn only on special occasions, and would be used at the sad time of burial, which was why so few remained as family heirlooms, unless the unfortunate owner had died away from home, or been lost at sea. However, such sad thoughts were pushed aside when the new garment was proudly worn by a bridegroom.

When the time came for Reuben to place the ring on Damaris' finger, her heart swelled with love, and her eyes brimmed with tears, for she saw that he had understood the significance of the simple grass ring he had made her so long ago. The double twist of fine gold shone in the morning sunshine filtering through the chapel window. 'Happy the bride the sun shines on', ran the old proverb. There were no two ways about it. Here stood one *very* happy bride!

Liz had knitted little Ben a new miniature fishermans gansey, and had traditionally blended the Storm family pattern with that of the Grangers, and he wore it with great pride. This was to be a special occasion for him also, for after the wedding ceremony, the Minister held out his hands to the child.

'Now, Ben,' he said, 'today your mother has become Mrs. Granger. She's not called Miss Storm any more. We think it's time that you were given your new name properly.' He reached for the small bowl of water that stood on the altar, dipped his fingers, and gently made the sign of the cross on Ben's forehead. 'Reuben Granger, I baptise thee in the name of the Father, the Son and the Holy Spirit. Amen.'

Ben touched his hand to the damp place on his forehead and smiled at the kind man who stood with his hand resting on the child's head. He felt very special, as Damaris had explained to him that this ceremony, just for him, would make him truly a Granger, and that he would have the same name as his father. He was very proud.

## 17

Isabella Granger sat by her fire, deep in thought. Since the birth of young Ben, and the prospect of Reuben's return and subsequent marriage to Damaris, she had been giving serious thought to the future. The young couple needed space of their own, as she was only too aware after the frictions caused in the Storm household during the long period of Jennet's convalescence the autumn before Reuben was caught.

Her sister, some years older than Isabella, living across on the other side of the village, was noticeably becoming more frail. Isabella felt that it was time that she gave her more time; her cottage was large enough for them both to have their own rooms; it was far enough from her own home so she would not be on top of Reub and Damaris, yet near enough to see her grandson as often as she wanted. Best of all, she would be helping the newly weds in the way that all mothers would have wished.

She knew it would be hard to persuade them, as both were, as she put it, 'inde-bloody-pendent', but using her sister's frailty as an excuse, she hoped they may see the advantages. Reuben had been brought up in the cottage, and it was full of happy memories, which had not been dimmed even after the death of his father. His older brothers were all married and settled, and she was certain that they would all be happy with the arrangement. Reub, as the 'baby brother' had always been a bit of a favourite with them, so no petty jealousies would be likely to arise. What better start could Reuben and Damaris have than to take over a home so full of warmth and love? Isabella was determined that they should accept.

After the wedding, they all returned to the Storms' for a splendid dinner. Isabella had already discussed her plan with Zack and Liz, so that they should not feel slighted. To her relief, they were full of understanding and gratitude, so that early in the evening, she called Reub and Damaris over and said would they come across to her cottage for a moment as she had something to give them. She smiled broadly, as they had no idea what she had in mind.

Much puzzled, yet excited, they followed her down the steep street, across the slipway, and up the steps to her own home. 'Set ye doon there,' she indicated the two chairs with plump and colourful patchwork cushions either side of the fireplace over which hung the kettle which was always 'on the brew' in Isabella's hospitable home. 'Comfortable?' she asked, reaching for the teapot. 'Happy?' They smiled and nodded. She poured the boiling water over the tea leaves and gave it a brisk stir before placing it carefully on the carved wooden mat Reub had made for her when he was a boy.

'Tha'll nivver knaw how happy, Ma!' he exclaimed, as he reached over and took Damaris' hand in his. Gently he twisted the new gold ring on her finger.

Isabella wiped a tear from her eye as she turned away and carried a large wooden box to the table. From her pocket she took a small key, and passed it to Reub. 'There, my son, is my gift for thee and Dam. Tek it wi' all my love, and be happy here.' Reub took the key and opened the box. Inside were the folded parchment deeds to the Granger cottage. The newly-weds looked at each other, speechless.

'Oh Isabella, tha can't do this!' said Damaris, when she had recovered from the shock of the surprise. 'Tha's far too generous, but, oh, Reub,' she said turning to her new husband with a brilliant smile, 'wouldn't it be wonderful! A place of oor own, and ti bring little Ben up in the place that was thy home! Oh, yes! Thank 'ee so much, Isabella!' and daughter-in-law and mother-in-law stood hugging each other, crying in delight.

'Well, now, what aboot that tea? It'll be reet stewed!' Isabella was touched to embarrassment with the display of enthusiasm from her new daughter. She set to smooth her rumpled apron, and poured out three cups of steaming hot tea in celebration.

Little Ben was so excited at the thought of having their own home. He rushed up the stairs, and climbed right up to the attic. Under the eaves which sloped down to the floor, was built in a small narrow bed. He climbed up on it and looked out of the tiny dormer window. He could see the sea!

That was his main concern, as the room he had shared with his uncle Matthew in Zack and Liz's house overlooked the street, and although he could hear the wind raging and the high seas beating against the cliff at the back of the house, he would have loved to have looked out, as Damaris had done in her own young days, and enjoy the excitement of a storm - from the warmth and safety of his own room.

Ben took stock of the rest of the room, and felt it was just perfect - only he hoped that Reub and Damaris would not think the same. This just had to be his. There was a neat little cupboard, and a bright clippie mat which looked brand new on the polished floor alongside his bed. It looked as if his grandmother had been busy! He need not have feared, for when he came down the steep stairs to the first floor, he peeped in to the big room at the front of the house, and saw his mother and the man he must now regard as his father, standing with arms around each other. They looked just as at home in this room, as he had felt in his attic. Shyly he crept into the room and wrapped his arms round the two pairs of legs.

'Well, Ben,' asked Reub, 'what dost tha think of thi new home?'

'Ah *love* it,' replied the child with emphasis. 'Can Ah have the attic jutht for me?' His gapped teeth still caused him to lisp. Reub looked thoughtful, and tugged at his hair. 'Well, Ah dean't knaw aboot that...' he began to tease the little boy, but when he saw the small face crinkle with disappointment, he immediately told him, 'of *course* tha can, Ben. Tha knows what, that was my room when Ah was a little tacker no bigger than thee. Ah didn't tell me Ma, but when t'storms racketed outside, Ah was for ever looking oot of t'winder, and mekking up yarns aboot shipwrecks and pirates, and that.'

There was very little to do to the cottage, as Isabella had looked after it with pride. The furniture gleamed with constant polishing, and the windows winked back the welcoming sun. The curtains were bright and clean, and even the lace edging which Isabella had added to the tablecloth was crisp with starch.

Because she had had no untidy menfolk around, with their muddy boots and smelly fishing gear, Isabella Granger's house was somewhat exceptional, and Damaris worried about how long it would remain that way, with young Ben and his little friends rushing in and out unthinkingly, and Reub bringing his rough mates in for a chat and a bite to eat. She shyly whispered her concerns to Isabella, who generously explained that it would be wonderful to have the messy men back in the cottage. That's what makes a mere house into a real home, she told Damaris. However, Damaris vowed to keep one front room as a special parlour, to which messy booted men would have no admittance, and where she would keep her treasures.

## 18

Reub's seaman's kit-bag had been thrown carelessly onto the bedroom floor, and left there unopened. He seemed reluctant to unpack it, and Damaris had respected that, knowing that he would come to it when he was emotionally ready. She believed that it contained not only treasures from his travels, but many memories as well - unpleasant as well as happier ones. Its contents represented five years of his life.

Later that evening, as they sat as a family before the glowing fire, she gently said, 'Reub, tha kit-bag. Isn't it about time tha unpacked it? Ah dean't want ti rush thee, but now we're settled intiv a new life, all that's in theer is in t'past.'

Little Ben pricked up his ears at the mention of the mysterious bag which had lain untouched on the bedroom floor. Unbeknown to his parents, he had guiltily sneaked the occasional prod and poke, and could feel all sorts of exciting lumps and bumps inside it. He had even lain down on the floor beside it and sniffed its intriguing smell of salt and tar and canvas.

He looked up at his father with a cheeky grin. 'Aye, Dad, *pleeease* let me see what tha's got in theer,' he begged, and his expression was so enchanting that Reub got up with a grin, tousled his son's hair, and agreed the time was right to make a start.

'Alreet, Ben. Go and get it. Is tha strong eneugh? It's heavy, tha knows. It's got a lot of stories to tell.'

Ben had not waited, but was already half way up the stairs. Reub glanced at Damaris with a strange look - half excited but half apprehensive, as if he was not entirely sure that he was really ready to share some of the harder memories just yet.

There was no going back, though, as Ben's plump little backside re-appeared on the lower stairs, one step at a time, dragging the bumping kit-bag behind him. He heaved it over to the fireside and dumped it down beside Reuben's knee. His small hands itched to begin untying the securing cord, whose knot had become almost too tight to undo. Reub's strong fingers worked away at the cord, and as soon as it had loosened, Ben's fist wormed its way inside. Reub put a restraining hand upon his son's.

'Now, Ben,' he said gently, 'this bag holds many treasures, and each one has a story. Some of the stories are of happy times, and some Ah'd rather not remember just yet. We'll tek it bit by bit, as Ah'm ready ti tell thee. Alreet?'

Reluctantly Ben agreed, as in his youthful impatience he wanted to tip the entire contents onto the floor and have a good rummage. Reub gently pulled Ben's fist out of the bag, inserted his own, and feeling around inside, selected the first of his treasures. 'This Ah bought for thee, Damaris, in Naples in Italy.'

Ben looked disappointed as his father handed a small package to his mother. 'Nivver mind, theer'll be summat in theer, later, for thee as well. This'n's got a good story behind it, and if tha'll coom and sit on me knee, Ah'll tell thee how we had ti fight pirates! How aboot that?'

'*Pirates?*' exclaimed Ben with a look of tremendous admiration for his father, and snuggled down to hear the tale as Damaris carefully removed the oilcloth covering and exposed a small leather box. Inside was a beautiful cameo brooch.

## 19

The frigate *Pelican* on which Reuben was serving his term of punishment, had been sent into the Mediterranean, to hunt pirates off the western coasts of Greece. Their main quarry was the schooner *Aphrodite*, Captained by the notorious Genoese pirate, Nicolo Siutto.

'Tha's heard me talk of Stoney Fagg and Smoker Browning, hasn't tha, Ben?' enquired Reub, as a puzzled look came over the little lad's face. Ben nodded, for Stoney and Smoker had been the legendary terror of the smuggling fraternity, with powerful ships, guns, and a complete disregard for the revenue men who pursued them.

'Well, Nicolo was a bit like them. He looked right scary, as he wore a black patch over one eye, and had an old sabre cut which had slashed his face, making his mouth turn up like this...' Reub grimaced and made a fierce face which made Ben giggle and hide his head in Reub's gansey.

The capture of the *Aphrodite* was a tricky business, for as well as a cargo of plundered silk, spices and money, she also carried a large amount of gunpowder. 'One false move, and *whoosh, bang!*' shouted Reub, 'and Ah wouldna hev been sittin' here now!' Damaris shuddered, but Ben looked on with huge respect.

'Anyroad, owd Nicolo's crew were not all as brave as he was, 'cos as soon as they was near enough land, half of 'em jumped overboard and escaped! We fired our cannon - not too close to *Aphrodite* as to blow her up, but near enough to let 'er know we meant business.'

Reub looked a bit thoughtful as he remembered the day he'd taken Matthew out to the *Kent*, and got caught up in the cannon fire that had led to Matt's own adventure.

'Aye, it were a bit dodgy, but we managed to shoot down her main mast. T'remainin' crew got out the oars, and tried to row her out of gunshot range, but we was too nippy for 'em, and drove 'er ashore onto t'rocks. We put out our pinnace and gig, to try and get close enough to board her and rescue some of the cargo, but them pirates were brave men, Ah have to give 'em that, 'cos they stood on that breaking deck and fired at our small boats. Ah hadn't been allowed to go, as Ah was a convict and might have run. Mebbe that was a good thing as two of our men were shot and it might have been me.

'Captain called 'em back to the ship, and they was nearly back on board, when there was this huge bang, and the sky was full of falling bits and pieces. A spark had got to that gunpowder, and that was the end of poor old *Aphrodite*. Pity, as some of that money would have been useful, as we'd have shared it out as a prize, and a bit of that silk would have made thi mother a nice weddin' dress.

'Ah well, some you win, some you lose. Nowt more was heard of Nicolo, but Ah've a sneaky feelin' that he survived, and mebbe he'd got enough of his money ashore to buy himself a new boat.

'Anyway, after all that, we were given a bit of an easier time, and sailed round the toe of Italy, and anchored in the Bay of Naples. Ah nivver thowt Ah'd see Vesuvius, but there it were, reet behind t'city. Ah nivver felt all that comfortable with it there, wonderin' when it was goin' to erupt again. Ah'd had enough o' big bangs when t'owd *Aphrodite* went up.

'Some of the main crew went ashore for a couple of days. They'd been away from home a long time…' he glanced at Damaris and gave her a knowing wink. She blushed at the thought of what those rough sailors would have been up to in such a port. 'Ah'd asked my best mate to buy me a little present for thee, as Ah wasn't allowed ashore meself. Ah said Ah'd pay him when he gave it to me, even though we was good mates, Ah didn't trust him goin' ashore with me money! Ah really didn't knaw what he'd buy, but Ah towd him it had ti be summat special, nowt cheap and tawdry. He did well… and this was what he bought.'

Damaris looked appreciatively at the beautifully carved cameo portrait of a handsome young woman with a dignified Italian profile, and delicately curled hair. It was a real work of art, and Reub explained to Ben how it had been made from a piece of thick shell and skilfully worked until the face stood away from the background.

Reub's mate had visited the tiny workshop in a narrow street in the old city, and had seen exactly how the cameo had been made. He knew that Reub appreciated a bit of good craftsmanship, and he enjoyed telling Reub how the shell had been carved.

'She's a very beautiful young lady, whoever she is,' remarked Damaris.

'Mebbe, but not as beautiful to me as thee,' said Reuben gallantly and honestly. 'Wear it on special occasions, not just for me, but for my mate. He was killed a few weeks after he bought that. I have a memento of him for thee, Ben. Ah promised Ah'd nivver forget him, and between us, we shall often think of him. Aye, he was a brave lad… but Ah'll tell you his story another time.'

Ben was quite content. He would go to bed dreaming of the swashbuckling Nicolo Siutto and pretend he was still busy pirating off the Greek islands. Damaris closed her hand gently over the beautiful cameo portrait and smiled grateful thanks to Reub. She knew that the mention of his friend had been hurtful, but perhaps the telling of his story to Ben would help keep him alive in their memories and would be part of the healing process which she knew Reub must now start to go through.

Reub sensed that his son had been disappointed that there was no gift for him, even though the story had been exciting. Reub had to put that right, so next morning little Ben came down to find an unexpected present. Reuben had bought a small model of a Mediterranean fishing boat to show Zack and the others. It was quite different in design from their own cobles, and he thought they would find it interesting to make comparisons. During the night, however, the little fishing boat had undergone some minor alterations. It now had extra masts and sails, some crude but effective small cannons made from scraps of firewood, and from the mainmast proudly flew a large skull and crossbones pirate flag.

Ben was thrilled and excited. Damaris smiled fondly at her small son as he rushed around wearing a knotted handkerchief on his head, and asked her to make him an eye patch, which he then complained he couldn't see out of. A bent piece of stick made a very acceptable pistol which magically turned into a cutlass, depending on the situation the young pirate was dealing with. He made a den under the kitchen table, from which he attempted to terrorise the household. Damaris pretended to be very afraid of him as he screwed up his face in what he considered to be a suitably fierce grimace and demanded that he now be called 'Nicolo'!

Reub found him an old fish box for a treasure chest, and a bit of strong rope with which to secure it. Thoroughly enjoying his son's games, Reub drew a map, saying he thought maybe long, long ago, some stranded pirate may have buried his treasure on Bay beach and it might be a good idea to go and dig. Father and son pored over the map, marking the most likely places with a big X. Ben shrieked with delight when he discovered buried treasure in exactly the spot they had chosen.

Reub just smiled, knowingly. It was such fun having a son!

## 20

The storm had blown up unexpectedly during the late afternoon, and by mid evening had shown no sign of abating. Reub got up from the fireside and opened the door onto the street. He'd planned on going to the Fisherman's Arms for a quiet drink with his mates, but as the wind gusted fiercely and wrenched the door from his hands, throwing a squall of icy rain into his face, he thought better of it, and struggled to shut the door before Damaris complained. Not that he was usually put off by such weather, but recently he thought he'd had enough and a cosy evening by his own hearth with his wife and son suddenly seemed quite attractive.

The sudden storm had brought back memories of a night he'd prefer not to remember, but he knew that he owed it to Damaris and little Ben to share more of his experiences during the time they had been apart. Tonight was the ideal time to share this one with young Ben, for the howling wind and battering rain provided the perfect dramatic background.

Reub returned to the fireside and lifted Ben onto his knee. 'Now then, little 'un. Art tha ready fer another story?' Ben nodded vigorously. 'Reet then, fetch t'owd kit-bag and let's see what we can find.'

Damaris swung the reckon over the fire, put the kettle on the hook, and blew the embers with the bellows. Next she took the long toasting fork from its place on the wall, cut three thick slices of bread, took a large dish of fresh country butter from the larder, and started to make the hot buttered toast which was such a favourite on cold stormy nights.

By the time her preparations were well in hand young Ben had once more struggled down the narrow stairs with his father's bulky kit-bag. Heaving it onto the hearthrug, he sat himself down alongside it and waited expectantly while Reub inserted his hand, rummaged about a bit and eventually drew out a small rectangular package.

'Reet, then, young 'un. Let's see what's in theer.' Reub pretended to have forgotten the contents, but Damaris could see in his shaded eyes that the memories were keener than he was admitting. 'Ah!' he remarked, as Ben carefully unwrapped a small but beautifully hand-carved box. 'Now that's a lucky find! Cos theer's two stories in theer. First one is for thi mother...'

Reub gently put his hand over Ben's mouth as the youngster was about to protest. 'Hang on, now. T'story of this box is well worth waiting for. Now, open it and give thi mother what's inside. Careful now,' as the small boy struggled with the tightly fitting lid.

Inside was a delicately wrapped package which felt very soft when Ben put it into his mother's outstretched hand. When she carefully undid the narrow ribbon which surrounded it, and opened the contents, in her palm lay the most exquisitely fine Maltese lace collar. It was some of the most delicate and finely made lace Damaris had ever seen - and she had seen quite a bit of the beautiful Mechlin and Valenciennes lace that Reub, in his smuggling days, had brought ashore.

None of that had been for the likes of her, as it had all gone to deck out the rich county ladies like the squire's wife. The exception had been the beautiful collar that the smugglers had sneaked ashore to adorn the lovely silk wedding dress that Damaris and her friends had helped Jiddy Vardy make for Jane Moorsom so many years ago, it seemed now.

A lot of tides had come and gone since then, and the carefree young women of those days had all grown up with their own individual responsibilities.

Damaris hardly dare touch it with her roughened fingers, and her eyes dimmed with unshed tears as she appreciated the hours of work that had gone into making it. Reub told her that he had bought it on the harbourside of Valetta on the island of Malta.

The *Pelican* was berthed alongside the jetty whilst the Captain went ashore with despatches for London. Reub had been leaning over the stern rail, enjoying the warm sun on his back, and taking in all the bustling activity of the busy harbourside. Reub had spotted a tiny, frail, very old-looking lady with a basket over her arm, pushing her way through the throng of traders trying to sell their wares to the sailors. There was something about her that caught his attention. She was dressed all in black, and although her face was wrinkled and wizened with the sun, and she had apparently no teeth left as her mouth was drawn into a tight line, there was a sparkle in her eye. Reub watched her for a while, then called out to her.

Gesturing to her to come closer to the ship, he indicated that he wanted to see what was in her basket. Leaning her head back and looking high up to the level of the deck, she began to spread samples of her wares along her outstretched arm. The hands that had seemed so claw-like and gnarled, suddenly appeared beautiful. By using sign language, Reub understood that she was the maker of this exquisite lace, and indicated that he wished to purchase something for his girl back home.

There were lace-edged handkerchiefs; no, Damaris would never use one of those, they were far too fine. A tablecloth, suggested the woman? Reub could not see that on their rough kitchen table. Finally, she spread out a selection of small lace collars. One of those would do very nicely. Reub could just picture that trimming up the neck of Damaris' familiar blue dress... or perhaps she would save it for her wedding? He got quite carried away thinking of the lovely girl back home, and became thoughtfully nostalgic. He could see the woman was beginning to lose patience with his daydreaming.

He made his choice, and putting his money in his neckerchief, threw it onto the dockside. He chuckled at the nimble way the old woman's hand shot out and caught it, and smiled as she tried to throw it back with his purchase tied up inside it. He began to be afraid her efforts would end with the beautiful lace falling into the harbour, when he spotted one of his shipmates bargaining with another trader nearby. Putting his fingers to his mouth and emitting a piercing whistle, Reub drew his mate's attention, and the sailor made his way through the throng to the old lady's side. She was a bit suspicious of handing the package over to a stranger, but when she looked up and saw Reub put his thumbs up in the air, she handed it over, and by the time he looked again, she had gone.

'That wasn't very exciting,' said Ben, disappointedly. 'Mebbe not,' replied Reub, 'but that afternoon, Ah felt so lonely and far from home, knowin' that at that partickeler time it would be at least another three years afore Ah'd be back home, somehow, ti buy summat for thi mother, and think aboot the day Ah'd give it ti 'er, somehow helped ti shorten the distance between us. So now, then, there it is with all my love.'

Damaris got up to see to the toast, putting a gentle hand on Reub's head as she passed, surreptitiously wiping away the emotion that she was afraid to show. She sensed how lonely Reub had been on the day he had bought the beautiful collar, and did not want to add to his distress.

## 21

'Now then, Ben. Let's have a look at that box. That theer bit o' wood has travelled thousands o' miles. There in thy hands is a bit o' t'owd *Pelican*! How aboot that?'

Ben took hold of the box, and turned it round and round in his small hands. It was beautifully made, with a well-fitting lid decorated in a geometrical pattern of chip-carving. Ben thought it was very special.

The howling gale had increased in strength, rattling fiercely at the window. Outside, the sea would be raging against the cliffs, flinging spray high into the air. Reub looked thoughtful for a moment, then he got up and reached for his boots and oilskin jacket. He also took down Ben's small waterproof and buttoned it close up around the child's chin. He pulled a warm woollen hat down over his ears, and to Damaris' astonishment prepared for them both to go outside.

'What on earth dost tha think tha's doin?' she remonstrated as Ben looked up at her appealingly. 'Surely tha's not tekkin t'bairn oot on a night like this? Art tha mad?'

Reub ignored her as he squatted down alongside the bundled-up figure of his small son. 'Reet now, Ben. Ah've a good reason fer tekkin thee outside. We shan't be long, then we'll come in and have some of that nice hot toast, and then Ah'll tell thee my story.'

Damaris shook her head in despair as Reub opened the door, the icy wind blasted into the room, and the two oilskin-coated figures went out into the storm.

Reub snuggled Ben's hand into his own warm one, and together they battled their way down to the slipway where the waves were roaring up towards them. Grabbing the child securely, Reub picked him up and ran across between the oncoming waves. Ben buried his face in his father's jacket. He was afraid, and did not understand what on earth he was doing here. Safely across the road, Reub carried Ben onto the high walkway in front of the coastguard's lookout. Here they were out of harm's way, but the seas still broke high above them, drenching them with cold salt spray. Reub put Ben down and put his arms round him, securely hugging him into his body.

'Now then, Ben. Ah've brought thee oot here for a reason. Art tha scared?' Ben wasn't going to admit it, but found himself giving his father a silent nod. 'Aye, t'power of t'sea is frightening even though we are quite safe up here. Tha must always respect the sea. Remember that, lad.' A huge wave thundered against the wall and showered spray over the two watchers. Ben huddled further into his father's comforting body. 'Ah have'na brought thee here to frighten thee, Ben. Ah just want thee to try and imagine what it would be like right oot there at sea, away from land and help, in a ship caught up in a storm much worse than this. Scary, eh?' Ben nodded vigorously in agreement. 'Reet then, now tha's got some sort of an idea of what it's like, let's go home for that toast and Ah'll tell thee that story.'

Awaiting the right moment to run back to safety, Reub and Ben dashed across the slipway, and up the long flight of steps which led to their home. As they re-entered the warm and welcoming room, Reub realised just how lucky he had been on the night of the shipwreck. He took off their wet oilskins, drew his son close to the fire, and chafed his cold hands.

'Ah had to do that, Damaris. Ah had ti mek sure t'lad would understand summat of what me and me mates went through on that night. Unless he experienced even a small part of that fear, he wouldn't understand what it was all aboot, and how lucky Ah was to survive. Ah nivver want ti go through owt like that ever again.' Fortunately, Reub was not to know that an even worse experience awaited him.

Ben was munching away on his toast, melted butter running greasily down his chin. He soon recovered from his fright and the discomfort of being cold and wet when food was placed in his hand. Reub accepted a large mug of steaming hot tea, and began his story. He took the box from Ben's knee and carefully laid it on his own. 'That box is made from some of the wood of the *Pelican's* topmast.'

With his mouth full, Ben asked whether his father had climbed up with a saw and cut a bit off. Reub knew that the lad was teasing and gave him a gentle cuff. 'Dean't be daft, lad! Ah waited fer t'mast ter fall doon onti t'deck!' Ben guessed that his father was getting his own back, and was now teasing *him*.

Reub then began to tell Ben and Damaris of the terrible storm they had been caught up in just off the Channel Isles, shortly after leaving the Mediterranean station on their way back to Plymouth for a minor refit and revictualling before being sent across the world to support Nelson's fleet in the West Indies. It would be a fine experience to go to those tropical islands, which most of the crew had never seen.

Those who had been, told of hot and humid nights under the stars, and beautiful and willing dark-skinned maidens. The men could not wait to get there, but their dreams were a long way off, that rough and dangerous night, and many began to fear that they would never meet those girls and would have to settle for what Plymouth could offer by way of female company.

The squall had blown up suddenly, just as it had that same afternoon, and from the warmth and safety of his cosy home Reub recalled how the *Pelican* had been tossed around like a toy boat in a bath tub. Everything that could be secured was roped down, but even so, below decks chaos reigned as all hands struggled to stay on their feet.

Those off watch duty had been flung out of their hammocks, loose possessions shot around the deck, and sea water poured in through the open hatch every time a sailor ran up and down the companionway to the upper deck. The one-legged cook tied himself to the side of his galley stove, and tried to catch his pots and pans as they rolled around with minds of their own. It was pitch dark on the mess deck as the galley fire was quickly extinguished and all lanterns had been doused for the seamans' even greater fear of a fire was paramount.

On the gun deck things were even worse, as the gun crews struggled to secure a cannon that had broken from its moorings. Men sweated and cursed as the cannon careered back and forth every time the ship rolled. Never did they have time to secure the rope before the ship turned again and the cannon rumbled away from them.

Waves broke relentlessly over the main deck, shipping tons of icy cold water as the bows plunged into deep troughs and then rose out again, shaking off the water like a huge horse emerging from a river.

The Captain's shouted orders blew away soundlessly into the howling wind, but all the officers and men knew exactly what to do without having to hear. In the top rigging and out on the yard-arms, exhausted sailors battled with the wet flapping canvas. With an enormous effort of manpower the main sails were reefed down, and just the staysails left rigged to try and steady the vessel and hold her into the wind. A keen watch was kept over the stern, where the unpredictable waves threatened to change course and swamp them. Extra hands were called to man the wheel to try and hold the ship steady. It was an unequal fight between weakened humanity and the unstoppable power of nature.

They had struggled against the elements for over six hours, when they saw, in the breaking light of dawn, a sight they had all dreaded… a line of white breakers just ahead of them. They were been blown helplessly onto the rocks in St Aubyn's Bay on the Isle of Jersey. The only possible hope they had of survival was to lighten the ship so that if the wind abated they could manoeuvre her around and head back out to sea.

Hatches were tightly battened, for if the vessel started taking in water, the weight would bear her down and she would wallow sluggishly and helplessly in the deep troughs of the waves. Rising above them would be an increasingly impossible situation. All hands were called to the pumps in case of need.

Reluctantly the orders were given to jettison the cannon, which they had so arduously secured. The exhausted gun crews laboured to axe away the ropes, and carefully timing the roll of the ship, carried out the tricky operation of opening the gun ports, levering the barrels off their carriages, and heaving them out though the open ports into the sea. This was a dangerous procedure, as if the ship rolled unexpectedly deeply the sea would rush in through the open ports and they would be swamped. It said a lot for the experience of the gun crews that they managed this manoeuvre safely, and a weak cheer of relief accompanied the splash as the heavy gun barrels plunged into the sea.

By late that morning the sky had lightened and the wind abated, and *Pelican* was able to safely turn and limp away from the angry line of sharp-toothed rocks.

On the main deck, a tangle of sails and rigging lay attached to the broken topmast which had snapped under the strain of the gale. The deck crew worked hard with the ship's carpenter to clear the debris and salvage anything that could be saved. A tidy deck was imperative not only to the efficiency of the ship but to the safety of her crew.

As the carpenter worked away methodically with his axe and saw, cutting up the broken mast to use as firewood for when they could re-light the galley stove, Reub asked for a chunk of the pine which he could keep as a souvenir of his good fortune in surviving the storm. The carpenter thought he was a bit crazy, but in respect of the remarkable seamanship Reub had shown that night under crisis conditions, he gave him a sideways wink and handed him the lump of pine. If they had to eat cold food because there was not enough wood to fuel the stove, they'd know who to blame, he teased.

Reub put it away in his sea chest, and in the coming months when they had long periods of inactivity under the sweltering sun of the Indies, he began fashioning the box which now rested on the knee of his small son. Of course, he reflected, when he was carving that box he did not know that he had a son, otherwise he might have worked his initials into the geometric design that he had chip-carved into the lid.

## 22

Reub told Ben how, after the storm had abated, the crew had made everything as safe as possible and began the long and dangerous journey home. They climbed to the top of the remaining masts and checked out the rigging, looking for any frayed ends that could snap and cause yet more damage. Flapping sails were reefed. Loose rigging, still attached to the broken mast, was cut away and tidied up. They did their best, but if another squall blew up they would be in serious trouble, as they had lost their main mast and there was no chance of repair until they made harbour.

Below decks, the chaos of flying pans in the galley, and sailors' personal possessions that had not been stowed away in their sea chests, created a muddle that would infuriate Captain Searle if he was to make an inspection. Crew members not needed on deck scurried about making everything 'ship-shape', as Reub described it to Ben. He had managed to create a picture in words that made a strong impression on his son's mind. He could really picture the mess as things flew around the deck, with sailors chasing after them and stuffing them into shelves and boxes.

Ben was getting quite interested. He wanted to know if they'd had a ship's cat, and if so, what had it done during the storm? Were ship's cats braver than house cats, he wondered? He knew that Jennet's cat always ran for cover at the slightest hint of a storm, especially a thunderstorm. Jennet's cat wouldn't be much good as a ship's cat, he commented.

Did it thunder and lightning as well on that night, because that would have been really frightening. His father could see that their little expedition together into the stormy night had made a keen impression on the small boy's mind. That had been Reub's intention all along, to make sure his son would understand the dangers he had been in. It was, however, still very different experiencing rough seas from the relative safety of dry land.

Ben wanted to know what would have happened if there *had* been another sudden storm? Would his father have been 'drownded', as he put it? His questioning mood was now well under way as his imagination took flight.

'Shush, Ben. Don't even think about such things,' cautioned Damaris.

'But,' persisted Ben, who could be quite tenacious for his age once he got his teeth into a question - Damaris had started to call him her little Yorkshire Terrier - ' if he *had* been drownded, he wouldn't be here now, would he, and we wouldn't be getting our presents?' Reub put a silencing hand on his son's enquiring mouth, and continued with his story.

With an anxious Captain at the helm *Pelican* had limped across the English Channel to the nearest port with a naval dockyard. The crew cheered as they passed Start Point and headed into the shelter of Plymouth Sound. They were safe at last.

Captain Searle was due for a spell of shore leave, and most of the remaining regular crew were also allowed to go home whilst their ship underwent a major refit. Reuben and the other five convicts posed a problem. They were still serving prison sentences and thus remained captives. Searle knew that Reub could be trusted, but the only thing to do with the others was to temporarily transfer them into the local jail. Searle called Reub into his cabin and explained the situation.

'Now then, Granger,' he said, 'you have a choice. You can be put on parole here on board ship, and take the job of ship-keeper while we are re-fitting. You are a capable young man, and if

I can trust you, you could be useful in helping the Mate to oversee our repairs. I think you know what the alternative choice would be?' The Captain looked straight at Reub with a stern face.

'Aye, sir. Ah do. Tha knaws tha can trust me. Ah'll stay aboard, Ah promise.'

'Well, make sure you don't be tempted to go ashore, because if you do, you can be sure you'll be picked up, and as well as being put into the jail your term of imprisonment will be automatically increased. Somehow, I think you want to get home as soon as possible?' he queried. There was no need for a reply.

'Now, as you know, I will not be sailing with you on the next voyage, but I will be rejoining the *Pelican* before your term is up, so, Granger, we will meet again. Your new Commander is Captain McKinley. He took part in the Battle of Copenhagen. He's a tough man, but fair and well respected in naval circles. He knows how to handle a ship bigger than this, and his officers are all experienced men. I think you'll get along with him alright. In fact, it will be a privilege for you to serve time under such a man. In future you will be able to tell your sons that you sailed with a man who had been one of Admiral Nelson's finest Captains…

'However, he will be bringing his first officer, Mr Adams, with him, and I warn you now, he's not a man to cross. He's one of the strictest disciplinarians in the navy, so watch your step with him!' Captain Searle warned. He looked as if he was about to say something more, but just cleared his throat and did not. 'You may go now, Granger.'

'Aye Aye, Captain, and thanks for the warning.' Reub had the Captain's permission to leave the cabin and went back out on deck, thankful that he would be staying aboard. He vowed to keep his promise as he respected Captain Searle, but he knew that it would be hard to be so close to English soil and not be able to put a foot on it. He was determined to be strong, as he gazed northwards and tried to guess how many miles he was away from home.

Little Ben was beginning to droop. He had sat silently on his father's knee, clutching the carved pine box, and now he was ready for sleep. Damaris closed her hand over the child's and gently removed the box before it fell on the floor. Ben was awake immediately, and made a grab for his treasure. Damaris smiled. 'It's alreet, Ben! Ah'm not tekkin it off thee! That's thine. Look after it well, and remember the story tha dad has told thee toneet.'

Reub smiled at his son. He thought he had made the box for Damaris, but now he knew he had really made it for his unknown son. 'Next time we rummage in t'owd kitbag, Ah'll give thee a treasure to keep in it. We'll have ti leave it fer a little while, 'cos Ah'm not really ready fer t'next story. It's a tale of great bravery and excitin' action, but for me it's a sad one, as Ah lost one of me very best mates. So, be patient, son, and Ah'll tell thee when Ah'm ready. The time to tell thee must be just reet, for this treasure will be a special one.'

Meanwhile, Ben was quite happy with his box. He had clutched it firmly and sniffed the resin smell of the pine-wood. The scent mingled with the smell of varnish and sea salt, for the mast from which it was made had sailed the oceans for many years. Reub was glad he had saved that piece, for a bit of the *Pelican* would remain for ever. When he went upstairs to say a final 'goodnight', the little boy was fast asleep, one thumb in his mouth and the other hand clamped firmly round the box. Reub's eyes misted as he touched his lips with a rough finger and gently transferred the kiss to his sleeping son's soft cheek. Oh, it was so good to be home.

## 23

Several weeks had passed since Reub had opened his kit-bag and presented Damaris with the Maltese lace collar, and Ben with the carved box made from part of the wrecked mast of the *Pelican*. Picking up from the last adventure, Reuben chose his time to continue with his stories. He had explained to Ben that he must wait until he was ready, for the next episode would bring back sad memories of a good mate who had been killed in a battle.

Ben thought it must be very exciting to be in a real fight, but Reub gently shook his head. The loss of any young life was distressing, and for one as promising as his friend, was doubly tragic. Reub was well aware that it could have been himself, and he supposed it was almost a feeling of guilt that made him reluctant to take up again his description of life aboard the *Pelican*.

He settled Ben comfortably on his knee, and began.

By the end of the month of the refit, *Pelican* was ready to sail. Captain McKinley and his officers had come aboard with some ceremony. The night before they were due to sail, he gathered the whole crew together and addressed them from the poop deck. He introduced himself and his officers, and told the men he expected total obedience, and attention to their duties.

'Yes, yes, we know how to run this ship, without you lot tellin' us what to do and how to do it,' was the unspoken attitude of the crew. They were experienced men, and knew the *Pelican* and how to handle her far better than this new batch of officers, who apparently thought themselves highly superior.

'Aye, Aye, Cap'n,' they all chorused obediently when Captain McKinley asked them if they all understood. 'Just let us get on wi' t'job, din't interfere wi' us, an' we'll get thee safely back home,' muttered the sailor next to Reuben. 'What was that?' queried McKinley who had ears and eyes like a hawk. 'Any questions, men?'

'No, Sir.'

'Right. Dismiss.'

There was already a sense of disgruntlement as the crew returned to their duties. It did not augur well for a happy trip.

As the warm July sun blazed down on the deck, they left harbour under very different weather conditions from those in which they had limped in six weeks previously.

Under her new command, the *Pelican* had a strange and unfamiliar atmosphere about her. Routines that the old crew had carried out without orders were now changed, and a distinct dislike for the replacement First Mate was simmering. He was an arrogant little fellow who found fault with everything.

Although a seasoned and experienced man who should have known that the regular crew of the *Pelican* ran the ship like clockwork, and worked their familiar watches as well-established teams, he swaggered about the decks, poking about and muttering under his breath. He apparently could not bear to think that the ship could be run without his involvement. Nothing pleased him.

Reub had watched him as he seemed to be forever picking on one of the youngest lads to join the ship. The boy had a look of Matthew about him, so Reub felt a natural liking for him.

One morning, the boy was scrubbing the deck, whistling as he worked. Adams strutted about importantly, pacing the width of the quarterdeck with an expression that indicated that he was the most important person on board. He really was an obnoxious little man, thought Reub and watched as the Mate silently crept up behind the lad, and with a sadistic smirk, deliberately kicked the bucket over. Reub suppressed a laugh as the dirty water splashed Mr. Adams' immaculate white breeches. 'Serve him right,' he thought.

Grabbing the boy by the scruff of the neck, the angry Mate hauled him to his feet, swiped him twice across the face with the flat of his hand, swore at him, and flung him back to the deck. As the lad reached out to retrieve his cloth, Adams cruelly stamped down on his knuckles. The boy screamed with the pain. Reub winced as he heard the scrunch of the bones, his ire rose in his throat, and he was about to grab the bully when he felt a restraining hand on his shoulder.

It was Captain McKinley. 'Mr. Adams!' he called, icily polite, over Reuben's shoulder. 'In my cabin, please. Now! And, Granger,' he added quietly to Reub, 'I saw that incident. It was, however, foolish of you to interfere. I am pleased I prevented you committing an assault on an officer. I am sure you know what that would have meant?'

'Aye, sir,' replied a subdued Reuben. 'And, thank you sir.'

*Pelican* was not a happy ship as she sailed into the Channel, although the sun shone, and the newly returned crew, apart from the convicts who had not enjoyed their stay in Plymouth jail, were rested and happy from their visits home. They resented the change in ship discipline, as they felt that they all knew *their* ship and her idiosyncrasies far better than the replacement Captain, and could sail her without changes in command. They were experienced teams and worked together well. They all hated the new First Mate, Mr Adams, as they recognised in him a vindictive and vicious bully, who had a disconcerting eye for the young boys on board.

Word had passed round that they were headed right across the Atlantic and south to the West Indies as part of the support fleet for Lord Nelson. Although this meant a long period of time from home, there was nevertheless an air of excitement associated with such a voyage.

Open grins lightened the mens' faces as they told of rumours of beautiful dark-skinned and willing girls and plenteous supplies of good Jamaican rum. Reub listened wistfully, as what would undoubtedly be an adventure and the experience of a lifetime which he would never otherwise have dreamed of, would still take him thousands of miles from home, and the uncertainty of a safe return.

As they sailed past the rugged tip of Cornwall, expecting the orders to trim the sails to catch the southward-blowing wind, suddenly orders came to alter course to the north.

The weather worsened as they ploughed their way into St. George's Channel. The crew were puzzled at this change of course, and disappointment at being denied the delights of the West Indies was all too evident. Captain McKinley decided it would be wise to inform his crew before mutiny set in.

'Order all hands on deck, Mr. Adams,' he commanded. He paced the quarterdeck as he faced a sea of puzzled faces. He explained that they would eventually be on their way to the tropics, but meanwhile had been given an important job to do, one which could well bring them considerable prize money. At the thought of having extra money to spend on shore, the crew listened attentively.

It had been reported that an American privateer had been causing a nuisance off the coast of southern Ireland, sending raiding parties ashore and stealing cattle, as well as harassing law-abiding trading ships in the Channel. *Pelican's* orders were to search out and deal with this pest. There would be plenty of pirates to tackle in the Caribbean, so this would be good practice, Captain McKinley suggested.

The mast-head watch was told what to look out for, and the very next evening a shout came that there was a vessel on fire, with a brig flying the American colours standing off from her. It looked as though there had already been something of a battle. As the *Pelican* closed in, the brig opened fire from a full broadside. *Pelican* veered away and aimed her cannon high, taking away some of the brig's rigging, then neatly changing course, *Pelican* sailed right across the brig's stern and fired a damaging broadside.

The vessels were so close that Captain McKinley ordered a boarding party. Shouting fiercely, the *Pelican's* fighting men swung aboard the American brig. Reuben leapt across with the Master's Mate, William Young. Ironically this was the only time he left the deck of his captivity, to board an enemy vessel. A fierce and close battle took place, which lasted over three quarters of an hour. Reub was not used to prolonged hand to hand fighting with weapons, and handed his pistol over to William, preferring to throw himself into the fray with his fists.

In the scuffle, a shot rang out, and Reub turned to see William fall to the deck, clutching his chest. Quickly butting his opponent hard in the stomach, he winded him sufficiently to be able to turn to William and drag him into the lee of the deck house. Grabbing the knife from his belt, Reub hacked at the tight neck of the Mate's uniform, to ease his breathing.

Cutting away the top button, he ran his hand down to the young man's chest, but his heartbeat was fading rapidly. Cradling his head in his hands, whispering words of comfort, that he would tell William's family that he had been with him, Reub shielded the young man as well as he could from the chaos raging around him. Only when the frightened eyes finally closed and the heartbeat ceased, did Reub reluctantly leave his mate and return to the fray. He wrapped the severed button in his kerchief and put it safely in his pocket.

Several of the *Pelican's* crew had been injured and killed, and the Captain of the American brig, the *Argus*, died later of his wounds. After the action the captured vessel was towed into port, and Captain McKinley gathered his crew on deck once more, to congratulate them on their success. They cheered when they learned that they would indeed have a share of the prize money. Most of it would be spent entertaining the dusky maidens of the Caribbean, but Reub put his share away carefully, along with the memento of his dead friend.

Later, he told Damaris when they were alone, that it was not safe to keep too much money in cash, as there were a number of ex-convicts on board, many of whom were hardened thieves. So, he told her, at the next port of call he asked his most trusted mate to go ashore and purchase a solid gold earring. Reub winked an eye and grimaced, asking her if it made him look fierce. Ben had already asked if he was a pirate.

If he had been able to go ashore himself, the jeweller would have done the ear-piercing professionally, but Reub had to persuade the ship's surgeon to do the job - either him or the ship's cook with a sharp skewer! It had been a bit sore for a while, but Reub could put up with that, he said. It would be a lot harder for a thief to pinch his earring than his loose cash!

Besides, he explained, it was a kind of insurance. If, heaven forbid, he had died in some far-off foreign country, the solid gold earring would provide enough money to give him a decent burial, and that was why so many sailors wore gold earrings.

Damaris shuddered and hugged him tight.

- 24 -

The autumn sun rose and cast a warm glow over the village as the low rays gradually brightened and poked their ways into even the shadiest corners of the cottage. Damaris had already been up since before dawn, making breakfast for Reuben and packing him up for the rest of the day. He would be away until evening fishing.

She went into Ben's room and pulled the quilt off the still sleeping child. 'Coom on, Ben! It's a grand mornin'. We'll pack up a picnic lunch and have a nice day out. We're goin' bramblin' then we can mek jam. Mebbe we'll tek some up ti Jennet.'

Ben burrowed back under the coverlet. 'No!' he exclaimed loudly. 'Not Jennet!' He was afraid of the old woman, with her strange habits and, even Damaris had to admit, a scary appearance since she had had her stroke which had left her with a closed eye and drooping mouth. Age had withered her face, she was dirty, her unkempt hair straggled untidily.

'Aw, coom on, she's a lonely old lady. She'd really like ti see thee. We could tek a bit o' fish fer the cat. You like the cat, don't you?' Ben nodded. 'And you like eatin' brambles?' Damaris coaxed. Reluctantly Ben got out of bed and slowly dressed himself in his knitted gansey, thick trousers and sturdy boots whilst Damaris busied herself in the kitchen preparing their breakfast.

Soon the smell of frying ham and eggs reached up to Ben's room. He sniffed appreciatively and realised he was hungry. The same smell had awakened Damaris and Matthew's appetites when they were children. Breakfast was always a good meal, especially when accompanied by freshly baked bread straight from the oven.

Reub had long since left to go with the boats on the early morning tide, and looking out of the kitchen window she could see them strung out across the calm bay, busy about their work.

She felt happy about going into the countryside as she knew that today they would all come home safe, and for once she need not worry about storms and rough weather.

Ben clattered downstairs and climbed on to his chair, now hungry and more enthusiastic about the day's expedition. He enjoyed brambling, poking about in the hedgerows, and cramming the fruit into his mouth until his chin ran with the sticky juice.

He liked looking for the small animals that lived in the undergrowth, and for the remains of the birds' nests he had found in the spring. He had enjoyed watching the parent birds, bright-eyed and wary, sitting so patiently on their clutches of beautiful sky-blue eggs. By now, of course, the eggs had hatched and the fledglings were well-feathered and enjoying the freedom of flying. Now that the nests were empty, Damaris would hold him up and allow him to see the care with which they had been built and lined with soft feathers or scraps of sheep's wool.

It would be a long time until they had to go to see Jennet, so he could put that to the back of his mind for now.

Damaris scribbled a note for Reuben, in case he should be home first, signing it with the initials 'D.G.' and adding a few x's with a smile. She thought of the childhood games when she and her friends had pared the peel off apples in a long strip, thrown it over their shoulders, and turned to see what initial the peel had fallen into on landing. It was supposed to represent the initial of the surname of a future husband, and Damaris always swore that hers landed in a 'G for Granger'.

She had already rummaged in what she called her 'avalanche cupboard' because everything always seemed to come cascading out onto the floor, and unearthed the baskets she always used. They were getting very shabby, as they were the same ones she had used when going brambling with Matthew when they were still both children. Those baskets had carried some wonderful memories of childhood picnics, and would carry many more new ones.

After breakfast, Damaris packed a parcel of the freshly baked bread, a couple of slices of the left-over ham and a big chunk of cheese in a clean white cloth. A couple of apples, a few pieces of sticky gingerbread, and a bottle of cold tea would make them a nice lunch, and they would find a good place to eat it. Damaris was happy at the thought of the day out of the house. Life was repeating itself, as she was now going on the same expeditions with her small son that she had shared long ago with her brother. She picked up the basket and a small parcel containing a rather smelly fish head.

'Poof!' exclaimed Ben. 'That stinks!' Damaris thought it would stink even more by the time it had been in the hot sun for several hours, but just smiled at Ben and said, 'but the cat will love it! The smellier the better.' She knew that cats were normally fastidious creatures, but Jennet's cat was so starved of luxuries, and had probably lost much of its sense of smell with age anyway, that the offering of the stale fish would be greeted with feline delight.

She closed the cottage door, and together mother and son set off up the track through Little Wood. The morning was calm with the pleasant warmth of autumn. The heat had gone from the summer sun, but they were still warm by the time they had climbed to the stile which led across the fields, even though much of the wood lay in shadow. At night it was a scary place, and not even young Matthew, with a teenager's air of bravado, was keen to venture there in the dark.

Damaris helped Ben over the stile, passed him the basket, and climbed over herself. Ben jumped happily off the lowest step, and then they were away across the fields towards Brocketts Wood where the best and juiciest blackberries awaited their picking. Damaris had brought with her the long stout stick which she always used to press the prickly branches down within their reach.

Ben shouted 'ow' every time a thorn scratched him, until he tired of complaining, and anyway it was difficult to shout with his mouth crammed full of fruit. Damaris smiled. Ben was eating more than he was gathering, and she ruffled his hair with a tolerant amusement. At this rate, she thought, he would not want any lunch. She was wrong, for Ben stopped cramming the fruit and declared he was hungry.

They found a good shady spot for their picnic, and enjoyed the good food, the peace of the countryside, and each other's company. Damaris was really taking pleasure from the day out with her son. Time like this, away from the village, was rare, and to be treasured to the full. A leisurely lunch over, the crumbs scattered for the birds, they rose to finish the task of picking.

Suddenly Ben stood still, rigid with fright. There was a rustling in the undergrowth. Damaris sensed his alarm, and put a hand comfortingly on his shoulder. They both kept perfectly silent, as slowly and uncertainly a hare loped out from under the bramble bushes. It stopped when it saw them, and looked at them with lopsided features.

Damaris put her hands over her face. 'Oh, no! Please, no!' she thought to herself, then realised she must act normally so as not to frighten Ben.

'Hello, hare!' she said gently to the animal. It continued to look at her in its disconcerting way, turning its head to regard her with its one greeny gold eye. Its white fur was mangy and scruffy, there was a dried bloodstain on its thigh, one eye was closed, and its mouth drooped to the side. When it eventually turned and loped away from them, Damaris noticed that it limped, just as

Jennet did after she had been shot by Ben Rymer all those years ago. She still walked with a limp for the wound had never healed in spite of all Jennet's medications.

Ben placed his thumb in his mouth as was his habit when upset or frightened, and buried his head in his mother's skirt. There was something not right about this animal, and it disturbed him.

'Has it been hurt?' he asked.

'Yes, I think it has. Poor hare!' she remarked, as calmly as possible.

From early childhood, Damaris had known that Jennet, the wise-woman, or local witch as most of the locals regarded her, had the ability to change herself into a white hare. Damaris had experienced this once before when she and young Matthew had been gathering primroses one spring morning many years ago.

That white hare had been in the prime of life, with thick white fur and bright greeny gold eyes. It had sat up and beckoned to them, and led them to Jennet's cottage, where they had found the old woman, breathless with running, sitting in her chair, regarding them with her own strange greeny gold eyes, and saying 'Welcome, my children. I knew you would come today.' Her power of second sight was scary.

Damaris took hold of Ben's hand, and together they watched quietly as the hare slowly limped back into the thicket. They listened as it rustled its way through to the other side, and they saw it making its painful way across the field towards Jennet's cottage.

The baskets were full, and Ben had eaten as many brambles as he had picked. It was time to make the dreaded visit. Together mother and son swung as cheerfully as possible, hand in hand, towards the tumbledown stone cottage which now seemed all too close. Ben clung to his mother and stared to pull back. 'Not going there!' he told her.

'Oh come on, Ben. Don't be mean. Poor old Jennet can't get out to pick her own brambles, and she'll need all these to make the special cough syrup she prepares for everybody's winter colds. You remember that bad cough you had last winter?' Ben nodded. 'Jennet made you that nice blackberry syrup to make it better. The villagers need her medicines, and we are helping by taking this fruit. Come on, we shan't have to stay long - and we have to give the cat his fish, haven't we?'

Reluctantly Ben walked onwards, still clinging firmly to Damaris' hand. They opened the rickety gate and fought their way through the overgrown herb garden, crushing the fragrant plants underfoot and releasing a pungent smell in the warm sunshine. Damaris knocked on the faded and peeling door, turned the handle and went in. Ben followed unwillingly, looking for the cat.

He found it laid on the bare floor in a patch of sun, and opened the packet of very smelly fish. Ben held his nose. That fish certainly did stink! The cat got up, and stretched tall on its thin legs, then crouched over the fish head with a loud and contented purr. Ben stroked it while it ate, then looked up to smile at Jennet for her approval.

The late autumn sun shone through the dusty window and illuminated her face. Ben recognised with horror the closed eye and drooping mouth he had seen on the hare. He did not understand. He just knew that something had frightened him. He turned and fled to the door, and stood trembling in the garden.

Damaris put the basket on the table, and said, 'I'm so sorry, Jennet. But I must go.'

- 25 -

Peter Maxwell stretched his booted legs towards the blazing fire and rested his feet comfortably on the fender. At his elbow stood, half consumed, a tankard of good ale. It was early evening, quiet in the bar as the boisterous fishing community had not yet come in after their day's work. Peter had established a regular routine, taking a late afternoon ride down from the farm, across the moorland track, then along shore when the tide allowed.

The Inn stood close to the dock where the boats were pulled up, and from the window he had a good view of the bustling scene which concluded a successful days fishing. Fresh fish was barrelled, packed in layers of straw, and crabs and lobsters crated, claws tightly bound with twine to render them harmless. The fishmonger's cart rolled up with a clatter of hooves, and the barrels and crates loaded ready for transport to market. The carter would drive through the night, often across dangerous tracks, so that the fish would arrive as fresh as possible for the early morning markets. The carter was an experienced man, familiar with all the moorland ways, and his knowledge had been invaluable on the many occasions he had taken more than fish on his journeys. When the work was done the fishermen could relax, and many strolled in for a quick drink before going home to their suppers.

Peter sighed as the last crates were loaded, the horse given a hefty slap on the rump to send it on its way, and the fishermen turned, almost as one, and made for the door of the inn. He enjoyed this quiet time, which would soon be disturbed.

The Fisherman's Arms recently had a new landlord, which was just as well, as Peter could not have otherwise comfortably made this his local after his retirement as a Riding Officer in the Preventive Service. He had spent most of his working life in the village, and although he was a government employee working against the smuggling community, he had still managed to be respected if not exactly loved by the locals - except one, he ruminated.

He closed his eyes, and the attractive face and figure of Jiddy Vardy took shape in his imagination. They had brushed up against each other - quite literally - in the early days of his appointment here and had developed a respect for each other which, now that he had retired, and she was not involved anymore in the village's smuggling activities, had matured into what was almost love.

His best mate and fellow officer of many years, James Herbert, had also retired, but he had gone back to his home village where he had taken over the local pub. Peter had lost touch with him, and did not know whether he had married. He missed James, and began to wonder why he, Peter, had stayed behind in Robin Hood's Bay. Deep down he knew the answer: Jiddy. He reached out and took another swallow of his ale.

Soon after retirement some three years ago, Peter had bought a small farmstead in a small village just outside the Bay. He had been considering whether to move to Gloucestershire where a small but pleasant manor house in the soft and gentle countryside awaited him. He would miss the proximity of the sea, but when he stood on the Cotswold hills and saw the long grass blowing in the breeze he could imagine the movement of wind on water.

The house was built of mellow Cotswold stone, which glowed in the evening light. Small-paned leaded windows reflected the warmth of the sun. It was a laid back and relaxed life, which he thought he was now ready to take up. There was a first-rate stable block attached to the manor house, where he could indulge his enjoyment for fine horses... he smiled to himself as he recalled how cleverly he had been deterred from buying Jocelyn Whiteacre's lovely horse, Firecracker. Jocelyn was a local country gentleman who had found himself caught up in a smuggling incident which had led to his horse being captured by Peter and his friend James Herbert. Firecracker was then put up for sale at a local auction. Peter had watched with amusement, and a little disappointment, when Jocelyn nonchanantly turned up at the sale, examined the horse and pretended that he had a weak leg. He then bid, and bought back his own horse, much to the amusement of Peter, who knew all along there was nothing the matter with Firecracker's legs. He was pleased Jocelyn had got him back, for he was a lovely horse and Jocelyn was a kind and considerate rider.

His deliberations reverted from manor houses and horses to the choice of a wife. Deep down, he had felt it was not yet time to leave Yorkshire; maybe thoughts of leaving Jiddy were at the root of his restlessness. He was still making up his mind when the small farmstead came up for sale. He went to have a look at it, and when he realised it was the very same farm at which he had first encountered Jiddy all those years ago, some voice deep down inside him said 'buy it.'

Leaning on the gate in the evening light, he pictured as if it were only yesterday, the vivacious and alluring young woman, who had audaciously brushed up alongside him, and deflected him from his purpose of seeking out the smugglers. He smiled at the memory and what it had led to. The cheeky wench had lured him into a moorland bog!

He wondered if Jiddy was also getting a bit restless here. She had a good living dressmaking, but now that her involvement with running contraband was almost non-existent, was there enough excitement for a girl - he re-thought the word and replaced it with 'woman' - of her vivacity?

She had come from an aristocratic Italian background, so maybe she would fit into the kind of county life he envisaged for himself. He also came from a good family, and had only entered Government Service because his eyesight had prevented him from joining the Royal Navy. This job did at least keep him close to his beloved sea.

He would have to sound her out, but if she agreed, they would each have to leave the village secretly and alone. Jiddy had been too big a part of this community for too long, and certain people would regard her marriage to Peter as a betrayal. Others would understand, particularly the Storm family, with whom he had established a respect and a kind of trust.

Peter finished his drink and called for another. As he drank it, he thought of the time he had cunningly kept the previous landlord trapped in the bar whilst his colleagues dealt with the smugglers who were landing barrels of brandy and storing them in the tunnel below. He smiled at the remembrance of the way in which he had spiked the landlord's ale, and thus made him helpless. Without a doubt, those had been good days, and he would have much to look back on, and maybe tell his children.

And with that thought, he found himself back with the picture of Jiddy Vardy.

Damaris was tidying up their bedroom when her foot caught in the cord that fastened Reuben's kit-bag, which had been stuffed out of sight under their bed. It was some time since Ben had asked to see more treasures, and Damaris felt it was now time for the bag to be emptied and put away in the loft. Reub had been home long enough now to be putting his past behind him and be looking forward to his new future with her and Ben, and his partnership with Zack.

She felt they had both adjusted well to his coming back home, though there were parts of his mind that she knew and accepted that she would never share, no matter how long he had been home. She realised that the old Reuben she had known since childhood was still there, but those five years had unquestionably changed and matured him, for he had seen and experienced things that would for ever be beyond her comprehension. She felt she had coped with these changes pretty well, as she had truthfully been terrified at their first meeting on his return.

She passed her duster over the already shining furniture, so carefully loved by her mother-in-law, Isabella, then stooped to gather up the kit-bag and take it down to the kitchen. She would take the lead when Reub came in, and tell him it was now time to open it for the last time. She hoped he would understand, and that the remaining items did not carry unhappy memories with them. To her relief, Reub was quite in agreement, and that evening, before little Ben went up to bed, Reub drew him onto his knee and put the bag on the table.

'There's three things in theer, Ben,' he told his son. 'Two of them's a bit strange, but one is quite beautiful. Ah'll leave that 'un till last.' Ben was impatient, and joggled up and down on his father's knee. He wanted to see the 'beautiful' one first, but Reub patted him on the head, and shushed him, told him to be patient, and reached for his kit-bag.

For the last time, then, Reuben untied the knot and placed his hand in the rough canvas bag. He withdrew a large, round object, and when he unwrapped it and placed it in front of Ben, the child's eyes widened in fright. It looked like a small human head, with hollow eyes and grinning mouth. Ben buried his head in his father's gansey.

'Tek it away! Dean't like it!' whispered Ben.

'It's alreet, it's only an empty coconut! Tha knaws, like when Matt meks a funny face in a tonnip fer Hallowe'en?'

Reub explained what a coconut was, and how delicious the flesh was to eat and refreshing the juice or 'milk' as he called it. Ben gingerly fingered the rough whiskery surface, but was still not convinced that it was a fruit. Reub explained what a useful plant it was. As well as giving food and drink, the fibres from the hairy husk could be made into hard-wearing matting. The trees on which it grew gave shade, and the leaves made the roofs of native houses. Ben found it hard to comprehend living in a house with a roof made of leaves. Didn't it leak, he asked? He thought it would be fun to live in a house like that, even if the roof did leak.

What sort of furniture did they have, he wondered. Ben was getting quite carried away by the idea of living in a native hut, but Reub said he didn't know as he'd never seen the inside of one, and besides, there were more treasures other than the coconut.

After his father's explanations, Ben appreciated the strange object a little more, but nothing could convince him to like it. To tell the truth, Damaris was not over keen on having it on the mantelpiece, looking at her every day.

'Alreet,' Reub agreed, the coconut could go back in the bag and live out of sight in the loft.

Ben looked much happier. Reub tried to describe the hot and humid atmosphere of the tropics, and how under those relentlessly blazing suns, day after day, he had longed for the coolness of the northern breezes of his native shores. Even the deep black velvet of the night sky could be heavy and oppressive with the threat of thunder, yet after the sudden tropical storms, which cooled the air a little for a while, Reub still often had a dull headache which throbbed persistently in his temples. He longed for Damaris' cool hands to soothe and stroke away his pain.

He took paper and pencil, and admitted that he was not very good at drawing, but made an attempt to sketch a few of the weird and wonderful plants and birds he had seen during his weeks in the West Indies as part of Nelson's supply fleet. Ben was still thinking about the native hut. 'Draw me a coconut tree house!' he demanded. 'It's a funny shape,' he commented, as Reub's pencil sketched the outline of the hut.

Although Bay men had travelled to the Baltic, and the Mediterranean, and even as far as North America, not one person in the village had seen the sights that had imprinted themselves in Reuben's mind.

One hot, sultry night, when it was too oppressive for the men to sleep below, his watch had spent the night on deck, under a blanket of brilliant stars. Although he was hot and sticky, Reub thought he had never seen such a beautiful sky. The air was still, without a breath of wind, the only sound the almost imperceptible lapping of the water against the hull of the *Pelican* as she lay calmly at anchor. The moonlight shimmered on the water, and he had felt so homesick, wanting to share with Damaris the beauty of that tropical night. He would never be able to describe it adequately. Suddenly, something flew off the surface of the sea and flopped on the deck alongside him. Startled, he picked it up. It was a flying fish, gasping its last breaths. It was such a strange creature, that Reub put out his hand and prevented his mate from throwing it back overboard. He learned that, with care, it could be dried and preserved, and now, that strange fish from the other side of the world now lay, wizened and brittle, on Reuben's kitchen table.

Damaris was not too sure she liked this gift, either, but Ben was absolutely fascinated and wanted it for his own room. He told Reub he would take great care of it, but please could he show his friends? Reub ruffled his hair, and said he could.

Damaris was now quite apprehensive what the last object in the kit-bag might be, but she remembered that Reub had said it was beautiful.

And it was.

In her hand she held the most exquisite conical shell, gleaming with the iridescent colours of mother-of-pearl. Whichever way she turned it, it shimmered, now shining pink, then blue, then green. It was truly a magical object.

Reub had been given it as a parting gift by one of the beautiful dusky-skinned girls who inhabited those islands - but Reub wasn't going to spoil Damaris' appreciation of the shell by telling her anything at all about its giver. Although there was nothing to be jealous about, Reub still did not want her to feel, at the back of her mind, that other loving hands had held and touched his, and that the shell held sounds and memories of another lovely maiden.

The girl, whose name he never knew, had held it out, and told him that whenever he put it to his ear, he would hear the sounds of the tropical surf surging on those white beaches, and imagine the clear turquoise blue seas and the glow of the moon through the tall palm trees. It would transport his mind back to this earthly paradise. Perhaps one day he would come back to her, she smiled coyly into his eyes. 'Perhaps,' he had replied, sadly.

Shaking away such thoughts, Reub smiled gently and held the shell out to his son. 'Put it against tha ear, and in it tha can hear the sound of all the oceans in the world!'

Ben listened carefully, and his mouth widened in a gap-toothed smile. He nodded. 'Yeth, I can. It'th wonderful!'

Damaris smiled also, and gently took the shell from Ben. Putting it to her own ear, she too heard the sounds of the tropical seas. This was the nearest she had been to sharing in Reub's experiences. To touch and feel was special, certainly, but to actually hear the sounds that he had heard all those thousands of miles away was something else!

Almost reluctantly she lowered her hands and looked at the object in her palm with a new kind of reverence and respect. Then she turned and put the beautiful shell in pride of place on the centre of the mantelpiece.

Reuben beamed with a contented pleasure. He knew he could listen to the sounds of those far away and magical seas any time, if he wanted to. But somehow, he felt he never would.

He tied the cord of the kit-bag for the very last time. He was finally home for good.

Part Two

The New Boat

## 1

Now that the priority of the wedding and setting up home was over with, Reub felt his life was beginning to settle on an even keel. It was time he turned his attention to his partnership with Zack in the boat. With Matthew now, hopefully, heading towards a career in the navy, they had to make a decision about their own future. Zack was getting older and less fit, fishing was a hard way of earning a living, and with the discerning eye of one who had been away from the scene for a while, Reub could see that changes were needed if they were all to survive.

Leaving the distractions of home and family behind, Reub took a long walk along the shore where he could be alone with his thoughts. He had taken the chance to talk to the other fishermen and from his conversations with Zack's old mates in the smuggling syndicate - Silas Biddick, Sandy Kellock, and Big Isaac McCaw - things were not too good for them, either. They were again entirely dependent upon the weather for earning their living by fishing from the small cobles, for none of them were keen to take the considerable risks they had once taken so frequently in the past.

Reuben now had the responsibility of a wife and child. Zack would be a little better off now that Matthew had left home, but Reub knew that Zack also saw that his aged parents, Isaac and Rebecca were kept as comfortably as possible. Silas and Sandy also had families to look after. Only Big Isaac lived alone, but Reub chuckled as he knew how much he enjoyed his ale!

Since the end of the war, when the formerly heavy taxes had been reduced, the old habit of regular smuggling was a lot less profitable. There was also a much greater risk of getting caught, as the many surplus capable seamen, no longer needed to man naval vessels, had been found shore jobs as part of the newly-founded water guard. The increased government presence in the coastal fishing villages was noticeable, and a definite deterrent.

No way was Reub going to push his luck and carry on with what seemed now to him, with hindsight, a positively blatant way of getting the illicit goods ashore. Although it would still be considerably more profitable than fishing, he now had responsibilities to his family which had priority, and which should not be jeopardised. Anyway, he thought, there would still be opportunities to make the occasional bit of dishonest profit. Even under these new circumstances, old habits died hard.

It seemed to Reub to make sense if all five of them were to form a partnership, sell their small cobles, pool their monies and invest in one of the bigger 'five-man boats' as many of their contemporaries were doing. It would, of course, mean more time away from home, and be more dangerous, as they would be away at sea from Monday to Friday, and travel much further out into the deep ocean.

On the other hand, it would be easier to continue to carry on a bit of cautious 'free trading', as the transfer of illegal, tax-free goods would take place further off shore and out of sight of the local preventive men. They would still need to take care on the landing, but felt confident that they could choose their moments. It all seemed like a very workable idea.

Reub had quietly observed several of these larger vessels riding gently at anchor in the shelter of Ness Point, the high cliff that embraced the northern end of the bay. They were graceful vessels, with three masts carrying brown-tanned lug sails. Once out at sea, the central mast could be removed to give them extra working space. On the deck between the masts they carried two smaller cobles, which worked independently of the 'mother ship', returning at regular intervals with their individual catches. Although the larger vessels looked sturdy enough whilst riding at anchor in the shelter of the cliff, the small cobles working away were very vulnerable. It all needed very careful consideration.

Reub sat down on a rock at the end of the landing scaur, lit his pipe, and gave vent to his thoughts.

It was a calm day, with small waves gently lapping the end of the rocks. The sky was blue and the sun warm on his back. He scanned the horizon, and contemplated the small cobles plying their trade. For a while, time stood still, as the same scene could have confronted him at any time over the past four or five hundred years. Those early fishermen would, however, have been keeping a wary eye on the horizon for the first signs of any intruders, as this part of the coast was still under threat of piratical attack. For that reason, many of the families lived a little way inland and combined a bit of small farming with the fishing. Then, over the past fifty years or so, the village had reaped a good financial harvest, as it was so ideally situated for smuggling contraband, with the rich rewards, but also with the attendant dangers as Reuben knew only too well.

Now, however, things were changing again, and a stark future beckoned, unless they could all pull together, co-ordinate their skills and resources, and hope that fortune would smile on their efforts to earn a decent living for their families.

To Reub, at this stage in his deliberations, there seemed only one way to go.

In all fairness he would first have to approach Zack as the senior partner in their boat, but he had had enough conversations with the others to sense that they would be in agreement. The main problem was that, due to recent anti-smuggling laws, they would have to licence the new boat, for it would be capable of venturing beyond the legal limit for inshore fishing. The law was supposed to deter such vessels from dealing in contraband from large ships which operated out of the sight of land. There had been a big fuss, Reub remembered, when the law was first introduced, because before it came into being, any vessel venturing beyond the legal limit was subject to capture.

The fishermen had strongly protested that this would seriously affect their livelihood as much of the best fish was deep sea. The new law, therefore, allowed them to be licensed to fish beyond the limit, but if they were caught dealing in contraband, then the boat would be forfeit and broken up, the contraband seized, and the fishermen heavily fined and put out of business. They would have to be extremely careful, or they could lose everything they had worked for. However, it would be hard, Reuben mused, for any of the new partnership not to be tempted to supplement their income, as all five had been hardened and experienced smugglers before Reuben's capture. A cruel lesson had been learned, and for a while they kept a low profile, but smuggling had been part of their lives and income for several generations, and it would be a difficult habit to break.

Reub sat deep in thought until the incoming tide washed around his boots. A flowing tide brought with it a feeling of hope, as the small waves surged steadily shorewards. Philosophically, he ruminated on the emotions of an ebbing tide, when the waves, in defeat, headed back to the open sea. Running away, he thought, but from what? Was the tide running out for him and his fellow fishermen, he wondered? It certainly would unless they did something to stem its backward flow, and they would need to do something about it before many more tides had ebbed and flowed.

## 2

$R$eub looked across again to where two or three of the graceful vessels rocked gently on the incoming tide. Rummaging in his pocket, he found a stub of a pencil and a scrap of paper. It was crumpled and not very big, but, thought Reub, it would do for a start.

He'd always enjoyed drawing so, smoothing the paper on his knees and finding a flat rock to support it on, he sharpened the pencil stub with his fisherman's knife, and licking the point, screwed up his eyes and began to sketch one of the boats lying at anchor. Often he would let his imagination control the lines of a drawing, but not today. He had to make this as factual as possible, as it would have to prompt his memory when he began to draw the large plan that he intended to produce that evening. It would have to be something really good, he knew, as on it would depend the success of convincing Zack that this was the only way they could go.

Even so, it could only be a suggestion of a plan, for the technical details would be up to the boat builder. There were two in the village, but only one who would be capable of building such a large vessel. Building the smaller cobles had gone on almost since time immemorial, and Reub's thoughts went back through time. As he looked across at the small boatyard poised at the edge of the shallow cliff, he imagined he saw the first Viking settlers, smoke rising from their coastal huts, and strong fair-haired children running about herding pigs. Maybe one of those eventually became his ancestor, for he had inherited the blond, blue-eyed features of the Scandinavian invaders.

He saw the burly arms of the boat builders emerging from short sheepskin jerkins, as they wielded their hammers and adzes. A distant sound of hammering reached him across the distance of the beach, and drew his mind back to his drawing. It still had the curving shape of the Viking longship, with a proudly rising prow, and a flat bottom with twin fins to assist beaching on sandy shores. The planks overlapped, clinker fashion, to give strength and keep the joints watertight. Ah, yes, mused Reub, those old Vikings certainly new how to build boats…

He shook his head and forced himself back to the present.

The drawing took shape well enough, and Reub looked at it with satisfaction. If, though, the boat builder could extend the prow upwards, like so… and even carve them a dragon head on the stem, would that not be splendid? Reluctantly he desisted from sketching in his idealised features, for there, in his hand, lay the beginnings of their new life, and he must be realistic.

He knew if he could persuade Zack, all would be well.

With that positive thought, he knocked out his pipe, pulled his boots clear of the rising water, carefully folded the paper and placed it in his pocket and set off back to the village to confront Zack with his ideas. There was a lightness in his step and a new enthusiasm for fishing that he had not believed would return to him. It began to really feel that he was back home to his old life, and that the past five years were receding into memory. He knew that they would never leave him completely, for too much had happened to him during those years away, but at last with this exciting plan, he was moving his life forwards.

## 3

Zack got up from his chair by the fireside, eased his aching back and grimaced as his knees clicked as he stretched. He bent and knocked out his pipe on the hearth, and wandered over to the table where Reub had spread out a large sheet of paper.

Weighting the corners, and smoothing out the creases, he showed Zack a detailed sketch of an impressive-looking three-masted fishing lugger. 'What's that then, Reub?' he queried, although he knew perfectly well what it was, having seen similar vessels anchored in the lee of the cliffs.

'Well, Zack. Ah've been givin' this a fair bit o' thowt lately. Ah can't see as how Ah'm goin' ti mek a decent livin' now that Ah've got a family. Ah knaw at present there's only me and Dam and Ben, but if he was ti have a little brother or sister - or two, or three,' he twinkled, 'then we'd have a pretty lean time of it. Ah've been havin' a bit of a chat wi' Isaac and Silas and Sandy, and they feel pretty much t'same. There's not the money in the old ways, and now wi' smugglin' too risky - tha can understand Ah've had quite enough heartache over that - winters when we can't get out ti sea in small cobles could mean very hard times. If we could earn plenty in t'summer, when t'weather is kinder, we could hev enough money ti tide us ower. We thowt if mebbe we all mucked in together and got oursens a big boat, that might be t'best solution. What dost tha think, Zack?'

Reub saw the excited gleam in the older man's eye, but it was quickly extinguished as he cautiously reached for the tobacco jar on the mantelpiece, slowly filled his pipe and lit it, to give himself time to answer.

When the tobacco was well alight, Zack removed the pipe from his mouth, and pointed with the stem at the outline of the vessel on the paper. 'Aye, she leuks well enough on paper,' he agreed, 'but how're we goin' ti pay fer her?'

'Tha means tha's comin in with us?' queried Reub, looking at Zack delightedly, and seeing the badly hidden twinkle in his eye.

'Why, o' course. Ah couldn't trust summat like this ti youngsters like thee and Isaac, not ti mention Sandy and Silas!' Reub gently reminded Zack that Isaac was almost as old as he was, nearing sixty, but still strong and fit. Sandy and Silas were nearer to Reub's own age.

'If we're goin' ti mek a partnership, Ah think tha'd better gan and get them reet away, and see how we can rake up t'cash!'

Liz sighed in despair, as she tried to push her way onto the table with a large pot of soup and a pile of newly baked bread buns. Men! she muttered exasperatedly. The table was covered by Reub's large sheet of paper, over which the five men pored thoughtfully.

The candlelight flickered on faces which expressed both enthusiasm and caution. Liz observed that Zack had a distinct twinkle in his eye, which belied the grizzled grey that was creeping into his hair and beard. She felt apprehensive, as Zack was not as fit as he used to be, and a project such as this was a big undertaking for a man of his age. She knew him well enough, however, to realise that whatever she said, he would go his own way, and looking at the expression in his eyes, she knew he would be going along with the scheme wholeheartedly.

'Aye, well, she leuks a grand vessel, Reub,' remarked Big Isaac McCaw, as he took a swig at the tankard of home made ale Liz had placed before each man. 'What dost tha think she'd cost?'

'Aboot six hundred pund.'

The men whistled. 'Phew! That's big money, Reub. We'll nivver be able to afford that. Not in a million years!'

124

'Aye, Ah knaws that it seems a lot o' brass. These big 'uns cost aboot as much as ten normal cobles. If we agree ti go intiv a partnership, and we each sell our present boats, Ah reckon we'd raise aboot half.'

'Aye, and then we'd need a load of money fer all t'gear. We'd need a hell of a lot o' lines an' hooks, an' bait.'

Reub looked thoughtful. 'Aye, when tha adds it all up, it's a tidy sum, even on top of what we can rake up oursens.'

Silas had been quiet throughout the discussion. He never said much anyway, but he was a deep thinker. He removed his pipe from his mouth, and cleared his throat, spitting into the fire to cleanse his mouth. Liz grimaced in disgust as the ill-aimed spittle splattered her clean hearth.

'Ah think Ah knaws where we could raise a bob or two.' The others looked at him in anticipation. 'What aboot asking t'owd squire ti lend us t'money? Reckon he owes us, seein' how much brandy we've dropped in his hidey holes over the years.'

'Aye, and remember that dress we got for his missus, not to mention that diamond necklace…' The acquisition of a beautiful French silk gown for the squire's lady had caused quite a stir at the time. To try and support the English lace and silk production, the King had placed a ban on the import of these luxury fabrics from France. The work of the lace makers of Nottingham and Honiton and the Huguenot silk-weavers of Spitalfields rivalled anything that was created on the Continent, but their trade was suffering because the county ladies were snobbish enough to want to flaunt only French fashions at society 'do's', and the squire's lady was no exception. To appear at a large gathering in a smuggled gown caused a certain pleasing frisson of admiration.

One Christmas, she had received an invitation to attend one of the top county gatherings, and had thrown a temper, refusing to accept the invitation unless she had a new French gown to wear. John Farsyde had pleaded with her that she would look beautiful in any of the gowns she already had, and would be a match for any lady there. But no, nothing would do to appease her, so he gave in and had a word with one of his Captains.

When the smuggling ship came into the Bay a couple of weeks later, John Farsyde had personally gone down to the shore to supervise the landing of the goods. When he returned home, he brought with him a small, carved wooden spice chest. The lady had been about to put it away in a cupboard to use in the Christmas baking, but on being persuaded to open it she found, carefully packed inside, a beautiful new silk gown trimmed with Valenciennes lace. She was delighted, and went off to her party as proud as a peacock.

'Well, we can but try. Who's gannin ti ask t'squire, though?' queried Zack.

'Ah says it should be Reub,' said Isaac, 'seein' ow's it's his idea.'

The four men looked up as one, and Reub could see he had no choice. Oh well, fair enough, he thought. It was his suggestion after all. He rose, folded his plans carefully and placed them inside his jacket, and made for the door. No time like the present, he thought.

Liz put a restraining hand on his arm, and gave him an enigmatic smile. There was worry in her eyes which she could not hide.

'At least have some supper before you go, Reub,' she begged. He could not refuse, and the six of them sat down to bowls of a hearty soup, which none of them really tasted, as they were all so full of the plans for their new venture.

## 4

After supper, Reub shrugged on his heavy pea-jacket, gave Liz a hug, and set out on the long walk up the steep hill that led to the next village, where Squire Farsyde lived in his beautiful Elizabethan house. He had plenty of time for his thoughts, as he toiled up the hill, down which he had rushed so many years ago, desperately needing to find help for Damaris who had been taken ill in the old churchyard, and instead, running full tilt into the arms of the village constable, who had been alerted to Reub's involvement in that fatal night's smuggling run by the traitorous Thomas Duke. Reub glanced behind him, making sure he was not being followed, though Thomas Duke had long ago left the village and had not been seen in the neighbourhood since.

He turned left onto the lane that led to Fylingthorpe, preferring to come this way rather than up the desolate track that led up from behind the village, and was used by the trains of pannier horses leading their contraband over the moors. In a short while, Reub knew that he must traverse the dark bend in the road, where he was in danger of meeting with Linger's ghost. Although he knew that the ghost was really a local farmer clad in a white sheet, making horrible moaning noises and riding his white horse to deter anyone who might interfere with the smugglers as they crossed this road on their way to the ancient trod which then led straight up to the lonely moorland, there was still a sinister and uncomfortable feeling.

The night wind rustled the dead leaves on the branches of the overhanging trees, and noises from nocturnal animals murmured underfoot. There was a thin moon in the sky, but it gave no comforting light, serving only to make the atmosphere even more eerie. Reub huddled further into his coat and put his head down, as he started to run. He chided himself for being so impressionable, and when a stray bramble caught at his jacket he shouted out in alarm, only to grin sheepishly and reproach himself for his cowardice. It was a good job he was on his own, he thought, for his mates would tease him unmercifully if they knew. Not many folk, however, would walk this length of road alone, he comforted himself, and whistling a jaunty tune, he quickened his footsteps and soon found himself well on the way to Thorpe Hall.

The tall gateposts at the entrance to the long drive up to the Hall were topped by grotesque lion-like stone animals. The faint moonlight only served to emphasise the fierce expression carved into their faces. Reuben gave them a cheeky grimace, straightened his shoulders, and purposefully strode down the drive.

He could hear the subdued murmur of the stream up which he had many a time waded carrying contraband, as it flowed through the wooded grounds. Glancing to his right hand side he identified the two tall beech trees, underneath which lay the well-concealed stone-lined chamber into which he had silently dropped kegs of brandy and bales of silk more times than he cared to remember. Yes, for sure, the old squire certainly owed it to him.

The stout oak door had a heavy knocker in the form of a lion's head, and alongside hung the wire cable which led to the bells in the servant's hall, to summon the butler to open the door. Reuben's hand paused on the lion's head, but he was reluctant to create too much noise. Instead he pulled on the bell wire, and listened as it rang in the distance. In a short while, he heard echoing footsteps coming down the hall and the door bolts being drawn. The door creaked open just sufficiently to show the butler carrying a lantern.

'Yes, who is it?' he enquired. Reub took off his knitted cap and twisted it in his hands. All of a sudden, shyness overtook him.

'Reub Granger. Ah need ti speak ti t'squire, if he's in.'

'What about?'

'That's my business. But Ah think if tha tells him it's me, he'll see me.'

'Wait here.' The door shut in Reub's face, leaving him in the cold, and with time to reflect on his purpose.

Eventually, the door opened again and the butler showed Reub into the hall. 'Take your boots off and leave them here,' the man ordered. Reub obeyed, and padded along in stockinged feet, following the butler to the door of the panelled room in which John Farsyde sat comfortably in front of a blazing fire in the huge stone fireplace, above which hung the portraits of his ancestors.

'Well, Granger. What can I do for you at this time of night? Sit down over there, and tell me.'

Reub was glad his mother had darned his socks, for it would have been very humiliating to sit in front of the squire with his bare toes poking out. Twisting his cap in his hands, he started, shyly at first, still overawed by the grandeur of the room, which he had heard about but never thought he would see for himself. As he warmed to his subject of the plans for the new boat, shyness vanished, and he unfolded the paper and laid the plans on the floor at his feet.

Reub was surprised at the calm interest John Farsyde took in his proposal.

'And that's aboot it, Sir,' he finished. 'Nowadays there's no way we can go on in the old ways. We have to move with the times, and that's the only way we'll all survive. Even if we was mekkin' same money through smugglin' as we did in t'past, tha must realise that Ah'd hev ti think a lot more aboot bein' so involved,' he added, breaking once more into the dialect speech which he had tried to modify in his approach to the squire.

The squire reached for the bottle of port which stood on a small table by his elbow. He poured two glasses and offered one to Reub. 'Not what you usually drink, Granger,' he smiled as he passed it across, 'but I think we should drink a toast to our new venture.' Reub did not miss the fact that the squire had said '*our* venture.'

'Come again tomorrow, when I've had chance to think this through, and we'll talk about the money. Bring whoever you like with you and we'll see what we can do. There's one condition, however,' he added, 'that you will still be able to supply me with the odd little luxury?' he added with a wink.

Reub hesitated. He really did not want to commit himself to the now greater dangers of bringing contraband ashore. However, he knew he had to agree, and hope for the best, otherwise they would not be getting the funding for their new boat. He paused for a moment before replying in what he hoped was a firm and convincing voice.

'Ah'm sure we will, Sir, and thank 'ee very much.'

Reub tugged his forelock as he rose from his chair. He was not sure whether he should shake the squire's hand or not. Seeing his uncertainty, John Farsyde stretched out his hand to Reub, and said, 'Here's to a profitable venture, Granger!'

Reub closed the door behind him, and rested his back against it for a moment, before the butler reappeared and indicated Reub's boots standing by the door. Under the butler's grumpy and watchful gaze, Reub tugged them on, and assuming as much dignity as he could muster, walked tall out of the squire's massive oak door. As soon as the door clanged shut behind him he threw his cap in the air, and with a whoop of satisfaction, ran as fast as he could back to the village to tell his mates the good news.

## 5

Liz received the news of the financing of the new boat with mixed feelings. She knew that this was the only way forward - the only way they could stay as a family in Robin Hood's Bay.

The old ways were changing fast, and one had to keep up with the changes or go under. It would be sad to see the old cobles go, strong and sturdy boats that had served them well. Most would be bought up by the older fishermen who were not physically capable of handling the big five-man luggers, or who could not raise the money for investment and who would end their working lives closer to home.

Perhaps, Liz thought, a little disloyally, their wives were the lucky ones! Their men would stay home. Liz wished that Zack would be contented to do the same, but she knew that he was fired up with enthusiasm for this new partnership, and although she feared for him, she knew she had to support the venture.

She would miss him getting under her feet all the time, as Damaris and the other wives would also miss their men, and they would live out the rest of the week waiting for the boats returning on the Friday. It would be a whole new, unfamiliar and unsettling routine. For a while, at least, the days would seem very long and strange, and the nights lonely and full of anxiety. It would be hard to visualise their men out on the ocean, at the mercy of the sea. They would not know whether storms threatened, or even if their men would be returning safely home, or whether the fishing had been successful so that all the effort and dangers had paid off.

When they were due back, a cluster of anxious women would be waiting on the cliffs, watching the tide-race between the scaurs, and holding their breath whilst the experienced fishermen safely brought their vessels in to the landing. Liz refused to think too hard about the dangers, but from time to time her memory forced her to remember the occasion when four of these same boats were overturned when in sight of home and safety, when a freak wave had hit them broadside on and capsized them. Fishermen, even the most experienced, were at all times at the mercy of the sea.

Perhaps, she half hoped, that the money would not be forthcoming, but when she saw Zack's enthusiasm and the way it lifted years from his expression, and he even seemed to walk with a slight spring in his step, she felt guilty and selfish.

That same evening the new partners were due to meet up to report on the sales of their cobles, and to bring the promissory notes of money so that work could begin building the new boat. Now that things were moving, Liz realised that she must accept and support, regardless of her own feelings. She knew Damaris had the same misgivings, and knew that she had to be strong for the both of them.

Zack was fidgety all afternoon, and only stopped wandering about and getting in the way when the first knock came on the door, and Silas and Sandy came in with big smiles on their faces. Silas felt in his pocket and produced a promissory note from the purchaser of his coble, but Sandy had gone one better. He had, figuratively speaking, already 'burnt his bridges' and sold his boat, and he proudly slapped a bag full of sovereigns on the table.

The chink of real hard cash brought with it a sense of realism, and when Big Isaac also came in with a bag full of money, they counted up and realised they had enough to pay the boat-builder to get started. Zack was to keep his coble a little longer, so he could continue to earn a living, and he would share the crewing duties between the new partners, so that they all had a bit of cash coming in. Reuben had contributed what he could afford from the rest of his pay, and Damaris had generously offered to work with the wives of Sandy and Silas at collecting the limpets and baiting the lines. It was to be a real family effort, and Zack and Liz now counted Silas, Sandy and Isaac as part of the new family partnership.

The new boat was to be built in the village, and little Ben wanted to go every day to see how it was progressing. He was disappointed at the seemingly slow progress, until Reuben reminded him that it was not like carving a toy boat out of a chunk of old wood.

The boatyard lay to the south of the village, close to the sea. The boat-builder had worked here with his father and his grandfather, carrying on a long family tradition. The smaller cobles were descended in shape from their Viking ancestors, designed for landing on shelving sandy beaches. Twin fins either side of a shallow keel kept them level when they landed. The design had changed little over the centuries.

Building one of the big five-man boats was a much bigger job. Not so many of these were built, so it was a matter of great interest for all the community. The boat-builder had become used to being watched at his work, but had to field off the many questions, or the job would never be finished in time.

Each day, Zack and Reub with little Ben in tow, would go and inspect the progress. The boat-builder took a little time off to explain to Ben how the boat would be built. He was a bright little lad, and maybe in years to come, he would be coming for his own boat. It was always wise to look to the future, and encourage new customers, no matter how young.

Reub showed Ben how the keel had to be laid, the ribs precisely shaped, and the planks for the hull carefully steamed and bent into shape. It was a very skilled job, but the boat-builder knew what he was doing, and Zack and the new crew stood and looked on with pride. 'Aye,' Zack would say, pointing with his pipe stem. 'Aye, that's our new boat. Ain't she a grand 'un?'

Ben showed such interest in the construction, that Reub suggested that together they should try to make a small scale model. Each day they went and made sketches, then in the evening before bedtime, Reub and Ben would disappear into his workshop, where Damaris would find them, heads together, cutting and sawing and glueing.

There was often an argument about bedtime, but Reub cleverly brought the evening's work to an end, by telling Ben that was all they could do until the glue or the paint had dried. He encouraged Ben to tidy up, and oil and clean his tools before putting them away all in their proper places. A real good craftsman would always treat his tools well, and by being tidy, would always know just where to put his hands on them when needed, Reub told him. Ben wanted to be a good craftsman.

Ben soon cottoned on to the fact that the tidying up could take a nice long time. Damaris would stand, leaning on the door jamb with a look of tolerant amusement, whilst Ben gave her the wickedest grin, glancing sideways from shadowed eyes. He knew that she was aware that he was putting off bedtime as long as possible. Eventually she would break the rule and enter the male-dominated domain, firmly take her son by the shoulders, and push him through the door to take him home.

The finished model was such a success that it took pride of place on the mantelpiece, alongside the beautiful tropical shell. The coconut stayed out of sight in the kit-bag in the attic, but the model boat became a family heirloom, representing what was to come... and what might have been, if circumstances had been different, and fate had dealt a kinder hand.

## 6

Eventually all was ready for the launching. It was a time of great excitement tinged however, with worry, for such a lot rested on the success of this venture. There were already four of these large boats engaged in deep-sea fishing, all of which were bringing in large and successful catches. Hopefully, the new one would do the same. All the family and friends gathered together by the boatyard slipway, each dressed in their best clothes. The whole village turned out to watch and a great cheer went up as the boat slid smoothly into the sea, and rocked gently at her rope's end until she settled. This was a key moment, to see how she rested on the water. She sat as calm as a seagull, part of the watery environment as if she had always been there. She was graceful and beautiful in her lines, and Reub cast his mind back to the day when he had sat on the rocks and made that first sketch. To see his pencilled lines taken shape in the finished vessel was really something, he thought.

He stood back a moment as Zack, Isaac, Sandy and Silas crowded round the boat builder, shaking him by the hand and slapping him on the back in congratulation. He had done a fine job, of which they knew he was proud. Then Reub moved forward to offer his own congratulations. It was a great moment in all their lives.

On the edge of the gathered crowd, standing in the shelter of the boat shed, stood Horatio Roberts and three of his uniformed men. He had already shown a keen interest in the building of the boat, poking around and being a nuisance to the builder. He felt a keen sense of responsibility to make sure this new long-distance vessel was not being adapted to carry contraband. He'd examined the laying of the decking, the thickness of the bulwarks, the levels of the shelving inside the storage hatches. Nothing had escaped his attention. Now he moved forward from his position, leaning nonchalantly on a fence post, until he closed in on Zack and looked him straight in the eye. Zack's expression never wavered. Neither did Horatio Roberts's.

So far the new boat had not been named, just the registration number had been painted on the bows. Zack had had something in mind for some time, but not until he had the full support of the remaining partners would he paint the new name on the stern. He would wait until they were ready for their first long voyage, and then make a bit of a ceremony out of the naming.

On the Saturday before the date decided on for their maiden trip, the families of the five men, again dressed in their Sunday clothes and gathered on the shore to admire the boat. They brought some food, and sat on the rocks in the warm sun to enjoy a small picnic. It was unusual to have time to enjoy themselves like this, but this was a special occasion and household chores could wait. The dust would still be on the furniture when they returned and the piles of ironing would still be there, but never mind. Today was a holiday.

Zack had been down to the boat early that morning, bearing a tin of paint and a fine brush. He would not say what the new name was to be, but just smiled and told them to wait and see. Now he was ready. Proudly he waded out to the boat and swung her round until the stern faced the excited crowd. Leaning forward, he removed the board that had concealed the name.

There, in gleaming white letters carefully outlined in gold, read the new name.

It was 'Elizabeth'.

## 7

One morning Matthew came home early from his studies. Liz sighed as she heard the door bang open. She was tired of telling him not to burst in like that, flinging the door back against the wall so that ornaments flew off the dresser and pictures slid skew-whiff. Admittedly, his attitude had much improved since Captain Emerson had taken him in hand. He was more polite, less surly, and certainly took more pride in his appearance. Liz wondered whether it was just the Captain's influence, or whether there was now a girl somewhere in the background. One thing was for certain, he would not be telling her if there was.

She turned to remonstrate with him, then stopped as she saw the expression on his face. It was a long time since she had seen him smile at all, and she didn't think she'd ever seen such a wide grin on his face as there was this morning.

He threw his arms round her waist and danced her round the kitchen. He'd never, ever, shown enthusiasm like that before.

'My, my! There's certainly summat happened ti mek him this happy!' she thought to herself.

When he could bring himself to speak, Matt told her that Captain Emerson had received a letter saying Matthew Storm had passed his first examinations with honours, and that he could now write to Captain Searle and ask if the place as Midshipman on the *Pelican* was still available.

Liz was, of course, thrilled for him, but immediately nagging doubts and a mother's natural worries clouded her pleasure. He would be leaving home; he would perhaps be sailing into battle, although things were relatively peaceful at the moment now that the war with the French was over. Then there was the financial worry about kitting him out.

A Midshipman needed such a lot of stuff! She had seen the lists when he had started to take his studies seriously. She rummaged around for the paper, which she had tucked away at the back of a drawer, just in case. She didn't really think she would need it, because at the time it seemed impossible that Matthew would be able to achieve his ambition, either financially or academically.

Now it seemed as though she would have to tackle the problem. Her heart sank when she found the list, smoothed the crumpled paper on the kitchen table and read it out loud.

'Three uniform jackets, an over coat and a watch coat, three pairs of white trousers and waistcoats, three pairs of nankeen trousers and three kerseymere waistcoats, two round hats with gold loop and cockade, one glazed hat, sword hanger and belt, eighteen linen shirts (frilled).'

'Frilled!' Liz smiled. She could not imagine her rough and scruffy Matthew wearing a 'frilled' shirt! Why on earth would he want *eighteen*? She shook her head and continued reading the list.

'Twelve plain calico shirts, three black silk handkerchiefs, eighteen cotton pocket handkerchiefs, twelve pairs brown cotton stockings, six pairs white, six pairs worsted, two pairs strong shoes, and two pairs light shoes.

'Why wouldn't his fisherman's boots do instead? Well perhaps not. They would look somewhat out of place with his fine uniform jackets and breeches!' Liz grinned in spite of herself at the picture this conjured up in her mind.

She read on; 'Six towels, three pairs sheets and pillowcases, two tablecloths about three yards long, a mattress, three blankets and a coverlet.'

'Good heavens, it sounded as if he was going to get married and set up house!'

The list went on: 'A set of combs and clothes brushes, a set of toothbrushes and toothpowder, a pewter wash-hand basin and pewter cup, a set of shoe brushes and a dozen cakes of blacking; a quadrant and small day and night telescope, a silver tablespoon and teaspoon, a knife and fork, a pocket knife and penknife, a log book, a journal with paper, pens and ink, and a number of suggested books including Robinson's Elements of Navigation and a Bible and prayer book.'

'Oh my Lordy! Where shall we find the money for all that stuff? Surely it's not *all* necessary? We've never owned all that much in our lives! Mebbe it's alreet for them rich fowks, but how on earth can a poor fisherman pay fer all that?'

Matt had rushed out to find his father and tell him the good news. Zack was with Reuben in the cellar sorting out a few old nets to repair, as the new boat was going to need a lot more gear than they already had, and that was going to be costly.

'Da!' he shouted, as he scrambled down the steep steps into the fishing cellar. 'Da! Ah've done it! Ah've passed me exams! Ah can gang ti sea after all.' He noticed Reub grinning in the background, and went over to him, threw his arms round his shoulders and said, 'Thank'ee, Reub. Tha's been a real mate, and Ah'm sorry that Ah was so grumpy when tha came home - but it had been a hard time, tha knaws.'

'Aye, Ah knaws, lad. But that's all behind us now. Tha's got a reet good future, and Ah think we have, an all, what wi' t'new boat. Times is goin' to get better from now on - fer all on us. Well done, tha's worked 'ard, and tha deserves every bit o' good fortune that'll come thi way. Good lad!'

The three men, for Matt now regarded himself as properly grown up, abandoned the old torn nets and closed the door on the problems, just for now.

Liz slumped down at the table with her head in her hands. Her eyes blurred as she read again and again the impossible list of requirements. How on earth were they going to be able to afford all this and have it ready in time? When she heard the men coming back up the stairs and sounding so happy - why was it that men never thought of the practicalities of life, she thought in exasperation - she pushed the list under the cushion, tidied her hair, and put a somewhat forced smile back on her face. She'd deal with this later, meanwhile she *must* share in the celebrations.

The good news soon spread for the close-knit community shared in the joys and sorrows of its inhabitants as if they were all part of one big family - most of the time, that was, unless there happened to be one of the petty feuds in progress. It wasn't long before it reached the ears of Jiddy Vardy.

Now *there* was a practical young woman if ever there was one. Jiddy instinctively knew that Liz, also the practical one, would be wondering and worrying how on earth they were going to kit Matthew out. She knew money was tight in the Storm household, and the new boat was not yet paid for. Silas, Sandy and Isaac had all cut down their visits to the pub in order to put more cash into the provision of nets and fishing gear. Jiddy was delighted for Matthew, of course, but his good news could not have come at a much worse time financially.

She waited until she knew the men would be out, then went around to the Storms' cottage. Damaris was already there, poring over the list with her mother. They both looked up as Jiddy entered without knocking.

'Oh, Jiddy!' she said, waving the list. 'How on earth are we goin' ti get all this tigether? It'll tek us years ti find all this stuff. Of course Ah'm pleased fer Matt and reet proud of 'im, but...oh dear!'

'Now calm down and let's have a look,' said the practical Jiddy. 'Well, now, we'll take it bit by bit. Has tha got a pencil? Right. Let's tick off the stuff we can rustle up atween us, and Ah think tha'll find there's quite a bit already. Then we'll worry aboot the rest.'

Systematically the three women trawled through the list, ticking and underlining. Jiddy agreed the uniform coats and hats might be a bit of a problem, but as long as they all got knitting and sewing, the shirts, trousers and socks would be no trouble.

Damaris said she and Reub had been given some towels as wedding gifts, and she was sure Isabella would have spare blankets and bed linen. Matthew had already inherited his grandfather's navigational books and instruments, and Rebecca certainly had more than one prayer book, and was sure to have a spare Bible.

Things were looking brighter now that the list had been reduced, and gradually the items were collected over the next few dyas and placed in the old sea chest that had belonged to Matthew's uncle. In the bottom of that chest, forgotten since the time he had been lost at sea, and which Rebecca had never opened since, there lay two navy uniform jackets. They were musty with age and not of the right rank, for Uncle Matthew had been a First Lieutenant when he died, but Jiddy pounced on them with delight. She shook them out, and although dust flew, there were no moths, thanks to the cedar wood from which the chest had been made. All they would need was a good clean and tidy up, a vigorous polish of the buttons, and some alterations here and there.

Fortunately the coats were longer, with enough material to cut down. She would check the style with Captain Emerson before she cut into the precious fabric. Jiddy was confident she could make them over, for a start at least, until Matthew grew and filled out, as he was certain to do. But they would worry about that later.

For sure there would be other boys on the ship who were outgrowing their uniforms, and be pleased to sell them on.

Thus, the daunting list had become, if not complete, certainly more manageable, as the women rose to the challenge.

Captain Emerson was very proud of his young protégé, who, after a few initial difficulties, had grasped the principles of navigation with a remarkably keen understanding. He was not surprised when the examination results came through, and Matthew had passed with flying colours. He was delighted for the boy, who was now on the first step of a ladder to what could be a splendid career.

The Captain stood with the paper in his hand, tapping it thoughtfully in his palm. It was great news, of course, but he knew that the family would not find it easy to kit him out. He would have to see what he could do to help.

A parcel arrived at the Storms' cottage a few days before Matthew was due to leave. Unwrapping it, he found it contained a Midshipman's hat. It was not new, but as he tried it on and looked at his reflection, he was delighted. He much preferred this to a new one, as it made him appear already a seasoned sailor.

It was a very different Matthew who, with straight back and an air of pride, stood self-consciously in the cottage kitchen on the morning he was due to leave to take up his first duties. All the family were gathered to wish him farewell. Standing patiently in the street was Rosie, harnessed to a small cart into which Reub had already loaded Matthew's sea chest. William Barnard sat on the driving seat, as Rosie was a bit fussy as to who held her reins. He would take Matthew into Whitby, to the White Horse and Griffin, where he would board the coach to take him up to Newcastle, thus reversing the very same journey that had brought Reuben home.

## 8

Gradually the new partnership settled into a steady routine. Early on the Monday morning after the naming ceremony, the five men said farewell to their respective families and started the short trek across the beach to where the *Elizabeth* lay resting on the sand. As they approached the slipway, groups of coble men left their tasks and came across to wish the crew of the new boat good fortune. It was a big occasion, not only for the new boat but for the community as a whole. On the success of each boat, large or small that engaged in fishing, depended the whole future economy of the village and its people. Times were hard, but the people were tough and resolute.

Liz would never accompany them to see them off. She could not bear them to see the worry in her eyes, so stayed home, busying herself with - she hardly knew what chores she turned her hands to - and could not have told what she had done, if asked.

Damaris and Ben led the donkey which pulled the small cart laden with the remaining nets and lines and baskets of bait. Ben loved the new patient grey animal which they had just purchased to help them carry their gear. It was stabled in a neat little shed alongside their fishing store and it had become Ben's job to go early each morning to make sure it was fed. He felt very proud of the responsibility and vowed that *his* donkey would be the smartest in the village. Damaris told Reub, with a sense of amusement touched with pride, that Ben kept sneaking off to the stable to groom it and give it tit-bits, and if they didn't watch it, the animal would be too fat and lazy to carry the gear or pull the cart. The donkey should have a name, Ben said. It can't just be called 'donkey'. He gave it serious thought for some time, when finally, in the middle of supper one night, he laid down his spoon, and without preamble, simply made the announcement; 'I've called the donkey Aphrodite!'

Reub and Damaris couldn't help spluttering with amusement, and Ben looked most affronted when they burst out laughing. *Aphrodite!* They had a donkey called *Aphrodite!* They'd be the laughing stock of the village. Ben reminded them that it was the name of Nicolo Siutto's pirate ship, and wasn't that a good idea? It would remind his father of one of his adventures...

Damaris, Ben, *and* Aphrodite timed their journey to the boat so that by the moment the men had all the gear along with food and personal belongings stowed aboard, the incoming tide would gently lift the hull. As soon as they felt her level off and move against the sand, they would raise the sails and carefully manoeuvre past the headland until they were in the open sea. Watched by a young woman, a small boy and a donkey, a new week and a new venture had begun.

When they had first started out, none of them knew how successful they would be, but so far, after the first few voyages, the catches had been good and enough money was coming in to start to repay the rest of the loan. However, there was still a goodly amount outstanding, as the extra gear had been costly, and the families at home still had to be fed.

The wives were settling into new routines, too. Some of them started going out as part time servants to the wealthy Master Mariners who were starting to build nice houses for themselves on the upper edge of the village. Some turned to sewing and dressmaking and some to helping in the village shops. None of them were used to being unoccupied, and so adapted into the new routines with enthusiasm, especially when they knew that the little extra money they were bringing home would help their menfolk pay off their still considerable debt.

So, life had moved on, and for several months all went well, until the boat builder now wanted the rest of his money. It was time for Reuben to make his final visit to the squire. John Farsyde had been kept in touch with the building progress, and had been invited to the launch, but declined, as he felt it more prudent to not appear to have too much connection with the new boat. This was a vessel that could, with care, bring him a steady supply of brandy and he did not want the village to know that he had loaned a good part of the money for the building. It was much harder nowadays to bring in contraband, due to the increased government presence on the coast. John Farsyde secretly admitted to himself that his financial help in ostensibly assisting in the purchase of a fishing boat could help him solve his own difficulties.

The kegs of brandy would be picked up from foreign ships well out of sight of land. He would have to keep a low profile when the goods came in, and not be a prominent figure on the beach, supervising the landings as he had in days gone by. He would have to sit at home and wait impatiently. The villagers were a suspicious and jealous lot, and his known involvement could bring trouble.

Reub was secretly relieved that the squire had not attended the launch, as there was a noticeable presence of the new Preventive Officers nosing around. Reub had observed a huddle of them standing in the background, muttering amongst themselves as the new boat slipped majestically into the sea. They regarded these new sea-going vessels with suspicion, for they were certain that some of them were already engaged in a profitable 'free trading' enterprise. The annoying thing was, they could not yet prove it. Zack knew they would be keeping a wary eye on him and his movements for a while, so was determined that they would not yet take any risks. They would land their catches of deep-sea fish openly, and even invite inspection if necessary. There would be time enough to pay back the squire with his kegs of best French brandy.

Reub waited until darkness had fallen before he set out once again to see John Farsyde. This evening he had taken the route across the fields, where he was less certain of being followed. The boat had been in service long enough to have awakened the interest of the 'snivs'. They had not found anything... yet.

Reuben had been nervous enough on the first occasion, when he had gone to borrow the money. This time he was even more nervous, for he knew exactly what the squire would be asking of him.

He straightened his jacket and smoothed his hair before tugging on the bell-wire that would summon the squire's manservant. He rather dreaded this interview, as he knew that once he asked the squire for the rest of the money, he would remind Reub of the conditions on which he had made the loan.

After what seemed an age to Reub in his anxious state, he heard the approaching footsteps and the squeak as the door opened to reveal the pale and sour face of the manservant.

'Yes?' he enquired abruptly.

'Erm, Ah'm here ti see t'squire,' replied Reuben, clearing his throat nervously.

'Wait,' said the man, gruffly, and shut the door. Reub shuffled his feet in the gravel until the door opened again, and the grumpy man indicated with a nod of the head that Reub could enter. 'Boots!' he said, and pointed to a corner of the hall, and in stockinged feet Reub padded once more into the squire's study.

## 9

One morning, a few days later, the squire's manservant called at Zack's cottage with a sealed envelope. 'No reply needed,' he said tersely. 'Just do what it says.'

Zack's heart sank, for he knew instinctively what the letter would be asking him to do. So far, the new boat had been very successful in the amount of fish they had caught, and the crew were now used to spending the best part of the week further out to sea. There was no question that this had been the right decision to make as money was starting to come in on a regular basis, and Zack wanted things to go on running smoothly and honestly.

Although he had been one of the most experienced of the old smuggling fraternity, and knew how to handle the old preventive officers, the new and increased government presence in the coastal villages was worrying. There were too many of them, they were all over-keen, and managed to pop up in all the wrong places at the wrong times. They were so numerous that they were able to run a rota system from their lookout in the newly-built watch house which was right by the slipway where the boats came in. What's more, they now had their own small cutter with a crew of six, so they could even intercept the incoming cobles before they even got as far as the landing. It was now almost impossible to sneak contraband in under their very noses.

The few places they could land were under the sheer cliffs to the north of the village, out of sight. The only way of getting stuff up the cliff face was to haul it up on ropes, and as the tide never left the bottom of the rocky shore it was impossible to land anything on a beach. The tide swelled in dangerously, and boats ran the risk of being wrecked on the sharp rocks. No way was Zack going to risk the *Elizabeth* by attempting landings there.

They could, of course, resort to 'sowing a crop', in which manoeuvre they would link a chain of kegs together, drop them overboard with a marker float, and be able to sail home and land without a trace of contraband being found. The tricky bit was to later carry out the 'harvesting'.

With a sigh he showed the letter to Reuben and the other men. Reuben shook his head. 'Sorry, Zack,' he said. 'Ah can't risk it, not now with a new wife and son. Ah've taken my punishment and Ah'm not prepared to sacrifice all that for t'squire's bit o' pleasure.'

Zack nodded. 'Ah understand, lad, but what's ti deah? Squire says 'e wants 'is brandy or 'e'll ask fer 'is money back, and we'll lose t'boat. We need at least anither twelve-month of good fishin' before we can say t'boat's our own. Ah knaw Reub had ti tell t'squire we'd get 'im 'is brandy, but Ah nivver thowt he'd be this strong aboot it. What's ti deah, lads?'

Silas and Sandy nodded thoughtfully, and Big Isaac removed his thick woollen cap and scratched his head. 'Nowt ti say, Zack. We've got nay choice. Mebbe it'll be jest this once, if we get 'im enough.'

'Reub?' Zack enquired, looking his son-in-law straight in the eyes, and challenging his loyalty.

'Ah'm not 'appy,' he replied, 'but Ah suppose we've no choice, not after all we've been through ti get this boat. However, Ah'm not goin' ti be t'one ti go and see t'squire this tahm, one o' thee'll 'ave ti go see 'im and mek t'arrangements. Nay doot 'e's gotten it all fixed up anyroad.'

Silas reluctantly said he would go, so he found himself standing at the imposing entrance to the driveway. All too soon he was nervously ringing the bell beside the big oak door, and waiting to be summoned into the squire's splendid house.

'Aye, tha was quite reet,' he told the others on his return. 'It's all fixed up. Smoker Browning is still working the run, and he's been towd ti - what big word did t'squire use - summat like rendyvoo - sounded French ti me, but he said it meant 'meet up' wi' *Porcupine* roond t'corner from Ravenscar. *Porcupine* would put in near Hayburn Wyke next Thursday neet, we would come in from t'south, out o' sight o' Robin Hood's Bay, pick up t'stuff, put oot ti sea and come in Friday as if we was comin in from t'north. Should look pretty normal as long as t'weather holds.'

He looked at Reuben's unhappy face, and gave him a friendly slap on the shoulder.

'Dean't worry, Reub. Ah'm sure it'll all be fine. We'll tek real good care. Ah knaw there's far too many 'snivs' aboot these days, but most of 'em are new boys, and Ah reckon we knaws t'coast a darned sight better than them! They's not gannin ti be trekkin' oot ti Hayburn Wyke on a midnight picnic, now, eh Reub?'

Reub shrugged. 'Ah suppose not - unless someone gets wind o' what we plan. So, not a word ti anyone aboot this, not even our wives - and', he added very firmly - 'keep oot o' t'pubs until we sail Monday. Tha knaws it's not that Ah dean't trust thee - all of thee - but tha knaws how it is when tha gets the extra pint o' ale, tongues git loosened.'

The men nodded seriously, taking no offence from Reuben's over-cautious attitude. They would all have done the same if they had undergone the punishment that still obviously seriously affected him. They would, however, have to deal with suspicious wives, who were used to their husband's regular habit of visiting the pubs on the Saturday night before a week's sailing. They agreed to meet up at Zack's cottage instead, supposedly to talk over plans for improving the boat. That should allay suspicion.

That weekend passed with a fair degree of tension being only thinly disguised. Liz was particularly sensitive to Zack's moods, and suspected that something may be afoot. However, years of experience had taught her to keep her own counsel and not ask questions that Zack would not be able to answer. It was with a mixture of relief and foreboding that she packed Zack's kitbag and food box, and waved him out of the house.

Once he had gone, she busied herself with unnecessary household chores, as she never wanted to watch him setting sail and heading out to sea. Some of the wives watched and waved until the boats were over the horizon, but Liz was never able to do that. She could not bear to imagine that that would be the last she ever saw of Zack. In spite of his annoying habits, she loved him dearly and theirs was a true partnership that had withstood the test of many years. She hoped that Damaris and Reuben would have such a marriage.

Out on the fishing grounds Zack's boat was doing well. They had hit upon a very rich shoal of herring, and the small cobles which travelled out on the deck were launched and manned by Reub, Silas, Sandy and Isaac, Zack staying on the *Elizabeth* to unload and pack the catches as they came in.

By Wednesday all the barrels were full, and under normal circumstances they would have left the grounds and sailed early for home. This week, however, they had to hang around for another twenty-four hours before they could head back and sneak into Hayburn Wyke in the darkness. Reuben especially found these idle hours of waiting intolerable. Moodily he smoked his pipe and half-heartedly whittled away pointlessly at a bit of wood until there was nothing left but an untidy pile of shavings on the deck. Silas had brought a pack of playing cards, and he and Sandy played noisy childish games, which nearly drove Zack's patience to the limit. There was a tension on board which they had never before experienced, and the hours passed unbearably slowly. Fortunately the weather was calm and the night warm, otherwise the lack of action would have made them all cold and even more miserable.

Eventually the sun rose out of a calm and sparkling sea on the Thursday morning, and Zack ordered the third mast to be reset, the sails raised and the rigging tautened up.

With Sandy at the tiller, they changed course and headed south, then lowered sail and drifted just out of sight of land. As darkness fell, they raised the sails again and headed silently into Hayburn Wyke.

It was a dark and moonless night, with no sound apart from the gentle lapping of the small waves against the hull of the boat. As they came close in shore, Zack lowered the sails and gestured that they should now use the oars. Wrapping the thole pins with rags so that no tell-tale squeak would echo across the silent water and give the game away, for one never knew for sure that they were unwatched, Reuben was distinctly on edge and reacting to every tiny sound. In the darkness they could still see nothing, and were beginning to think that they had beaten the *Porcupine* to the rendezvous.

Suddenly, Zack felt a tug on his gansey sleeve, and Silas pointed directly ahead to where a huge black shape loomed out of the darkness. They were almost on top of the *Porcupine*, but Smoker had cleverly disguised his vessel with a very large quantity of black paint. Even the furled sails had been dyed black, and the deck planks tarred.

The only glimmer of lightness came from the faces of the crew as they gathered over the stern to watch Zack come alongside. Reuben was quite surprised that Smoker had not insisted that his crew had disguised their faces with a vigorous application of burnt cork!

One dim lantern was carefully lowered over the side into Zack's boat so that he could see where to stow the four dozen small black-tarred kegs under his fishing gear. He was a little alarmed that there should have been so many of them, but, Smoker whispered, that was what the squire had ordered, and that was what he expected to get. As long as they could keep it well hidden and organise an efficient unloading, that would be that.

Bidding Smoker farewell, Zack carefully guided the *Elizabeth* out of the creek and back out to sea. He was thankful that it was a calm night, for he felt the boat to be too heavily laden and unbalanced. The waterline appeared uncomfortably close.

The next worry was getting ashore. They hadn't really thought that through, so the rest of the night was spent in discussing plans. Silas suggested that if they timed their arrival at low tide, then one of them could row ashore in the dinghy whilst the boat anchored in deeper water to await the flowing tide to take them in shore. Silas would meanwhile organise the horse-drawn carts they normally used to land their catch and fishing gear, which had then to be driven up the slipway right under the windows of the watch house. He would then need to drop a hint that something funny was going on down the beach to the south - a ruse that would, with a bit of luck, lead to the abandonment of the watch keeper and the organising of the preventive men to go and investigate. They had used this sort of misinformation many times in the past, but the old experienced officers were uncomfortably suspicious, and now checked out any rumours before heading off on wild goose chases. These new young ones should be easier to fool, Silas thought hopefully, as he rowed ashore. This, however, was a dangerous supposition.

## 10

William Barnard gently drew on the traces of Rosie, his big white carthorse. 'Whoa there, girl,' he said, slapping the reins gently on her back. She knew the signal, and willingly stopped. He walked round from the handle of the plough, scratched her between the ears and patted her on the nose. 'Time for a break.' Rosie tossed her head and whinnied in appreciation.

William unhitched the harness, hooked Rosie's nosebag over her head and led her munching contentedly to the shade of the big oak tree in the corner of the field they had been ploughing. He looked across the straight furrows with pride, and smiled at the flocks of opportunist seagulls which had swooped down on the newly turned earth. Apart from being the wrong colour, William thought, they could well be foraging on the waves of the sea, which he could hear breaking against the cliffs not far from where he was working.

The sound and smell of the sea was never very far away and even on the hottest summer day a gentle breeze wafted up the cliff face and across the cornfield. It would be well into another year before the wheat, which was due to be sown after he had finished the ploughing, would grow and ripen ready for harvest. The seasons of the farm continued as they had for generations, and William was content with his lot.

Farming had its ups and downs, of course, according to the whims of the weather, but he a lot more secure than his fisherman friends. He had a good life, a happy home, a beautiful wife and two lovely healthy sons, and before many more weeks were out, he would have another son... or perhaps a daughter. Yes, a little girl would be very nice, and would be company for Jane. His mother, Sarah, would dote on a granddaughter.

He hitched Rosie to the tree, but it was an unnecessary action as she never had the urge to wander off, but stood happily, one hoof raised onto its point, her rump relaxed as she enjoyed her food. Later, when he had finished his own lunch, William would treat her to the core of his apple. He loved to see the juice run down her hairy chin as she munched with her big strong yellow teeth. He indulged her with a vigorous scratching between her ears, and talked to her as if she understood all he was saying. She certainly nodded her head from time to time in agreement.

She was a good mate as well as a good workhorse, was Rosie. When she had drawn the decorated wagon that had carried William and his new bride from the church after heir wedding, she had been groomed to a glossy sheen, her fetlocks brushed until they were like silk, and her hooves oiled until they shone like the finest polished wood.

The choice of Jane Moorsom for a wife had been a good one. Not only was she pretty - nay, beautiful - William corrected himself, but she had adapted into the lives of his farming family as if she had been born to it, instead of being the daughter of one of the fishermen who had lived in the old village of Bay. She was loved by both his father and his mother, who regarded her as the daughter they had never been fortunate to have. A houseful of strong and healthy boys was wonderful for a farming family, but being set out in the countryside with no immediate neighbours with whom she could have a good gossip, Sarah Barnard was delighted with the company and humour young Jane had brought into the household.

William moved away from the horse, chose a nice spot under the shady tree, and was about to sit down and open his lunch box, when the noise of children happily shouting echoed above the sound of the distant sea. Looking up, William smiled to see his two small sturdy sons scrambling across the unploughed earth, with their mother struggling some way behind them. She was heavily pregnant, and bore a weighty basket on her arm. Jane paused, wiped her forehead, and rested her load for a moment on the ground.

William ran to welcome her and relieve her of the load. His two boys flung themselves round his legs in greeting, then grabbed his lunch box and shot off under a hedge with their plunder. 'Hey, lads, that's me dinner!' he remonstrated, but the boys took no notice and settled down to uncover their booty.

Jane kissed him, and uncovered the basket. Inside, wrapped in a clean red and white checked cloth, was a hot, steaming meat pie, fresh from the oven, newly-baked bread rolls, a large pat of  glistening country butter and several jars of refreshing cold tea. 'My, tha'rt a rescuing angel. Ah could murder a bit o' that pie!'

Looking across at his sons, guzzling away in the shade of the tall hawthorn hedge, twisted and bent permanently landwards from the strength of the persistent sea winds, he grinned and remarked, 'Jest leuk at the greedy little beggars. Dean't let 'em get a whiff o'this pie!'

He shielded the food with his strong hands, and carefully bit into the delicious pastry. Jane leant forward to mop the trace of gravy that was escaping down his chin. She looked up from under the brim of her cotton countrywoman's bonnet and smiled her wonderful smile that never failed to turn his guts to water. He was so lucky.

But, he had to admit, Jane had been lucky, too. He reckoned he was not a bad catch, being strong and handsome - the thought made him straighten his neckerchief self-consciously - and she had come into a family where she was dearly loved. She also, unlike Damaris, had the support of a husband when her children were born, and she looked forward to the arrival of her third.

Jane looked over with an indulgent smile at her two young rascals devouring their father's lunch, and hoped secretly that the child she was carrying now would be a daughter. She understood how Sarah had felt with her houseful of boys, and how nice it would be to teach a girl to bake and sew and look after her menfolk, as well as giving the sort of companionship a mother should have with a daughter. Certainly, Jane was lucky, too.

Jane was not the only lucky female that afternoon, for William was so full of his pie that he had no room for his apple, and Rosie got an unexpected treat.

Lunch-break over, Jane and the boys tidied up the remains of the lunch, scattering the crumbs for the birds, and carefully packing the dishes, returned to the farm. William roused Rosie from her reverie, and man and horse got back to work. Ploughing was a lonely and boring job; Rosie was such an expert that all William had to do was to keep a grip on the handles of the plough. She kept a wonderfully straight furrow without the help of 'her' man. There was plenty of time for thinking.

William was in the mood for reminiscing, and as he plodded behind the plough, thought over with amusement some of the events he had been involved with when his father was still part of the local smuggling fraternity...

The night, for instance, when Samuel had been awakened by a very angry Stoney Fagg because he had mistaken the date of the arrival of the smuggling lugger, and had not got the fleeces shorn from his sheep to smuggle back to France, and they had had to wake Seth the shepherd and get the whole flock secretly down to the shore and on board the *Kent* in pitch darkness, was never to be

156

forgotten. Sheep were not exactly the quietest and most discreet of animals, especially when woken up in the middle of the night, and herded down a cliff!

Neither was the occasion when Samuel had found a stray keg of brandy floating in on the tide, and taken it up to the farmhouse. They had just emptied the contents into a milk churn, and replaced it with water, when Riding Officers Peter Maxwell and James Herbert had rushed into the farmhouse kitchen, because they, too, had seen the keg floating ashore, and followed Sam up to the farm in order to capture it and make a bit of profit for themselves. Sam and the family had chuckled over the incident for a long time, especially as it had been a very hot evening, and the officers had carried the very heavy keg all the way to Whitby, only to find it was filled with water!

William had got this far in his reminiscences when the turn of the furrow led him close to the cliff edge. Something made him pause, and telling Rosie to 'Stand, girl,' he parted the bushes and peered down on to the beach below.

Earlier in the afternoon he had witnessed what he thought was Zack's new boat moored alongside the Landing to unload his week's catch of fish. Barrels of herring stood on the flat rocks alongside the boat, and Reuben had been making his way back towards the slipway with his horse and cart with a load of fish boxes. A couple of the newly appointed Revenue men had stood by, watching. They had been keeping an uncomfortably wary eye on the *Elizabeth*, ever since she had been on the boatbuilder's stocks.

So far, they had found nothing, but even so, Reub had, with beating heart, doffed his cap to them as they approached the cart and had a cursory look at its contents. Reub knew he need not worry as all he was carrying was genuine fish, but a close inspection of the boat would not look so innocent. The rest of the *Elizabeth's* cargo would be unloaded later - elsewhere.

Now, as evening was falling, and William was about to make the last turn before calling it a day, his attention was attracted by a group of Revenue men heading along the shore towards Ravenscar. William smiled to himself; he'd seen it all before. It was fairly easy to con a new bunch of men into believing carefully spread rumours that a run of contraband was due in later that night, to be landed on the little jetty that the alum workers used just below the foot of the cliffs of Raven Hill.

It was far enough from the village of Robin Hood's Bay for the officers not to be able to see what was going on in the village - especially when it would be dark - and usually these decoys were planned so that the officers would be trapped by the incoming tide, and unable to get back to the Bay until the next morning. They could, of course, have made the undignified scramble up the steep cliff and sought the cliff top path, but at night, even with lanterns, this was treacherous, as the soft clay was subject to sudden erosion and collapse.

William chuckled, turned back to the patiently waiting Rosie, ruffled her forelock, slapped her gently on the rump and said, 'Come on, girl. That's enough for today. How about a nice rub down and some supper?'

Was it imagination, or did Rosie have a skittishness about her step as she and William turned for home?

## - 11 -

The *Elizabeth* lay off the Landing until the tide was right to bring her alongside to start unloading. Silas was there, ready with three carts and a team of helpers. Steadily they worked, unloading the barrels and fish boxes, but being careful not to disturb the kegs of brandy which lay neatly stacked below the nets. As soon as the last box had been loaded onto the cart, Silas gave his place at the horse's head to Reub and quickly climbed back on board. So far, so good. They had not attracted the attention of the Revenue men. Silas was keen to put back out to sea before they noticed anything suspicious. It was an anxious time.

He had indicated that arrangements were in place for the landing of the kegs once darkness had fallen. The boat would have anchored under the cliffs, inside the small cove which lay just to the north of the village. A row of cottages perched precariously close to the cliff edge, and the plan was that the landing team would stand ready with ropes, to haul the cargo up the cliff face and spirit the barrels away into the cellar of the Mariners Tavern. It had been done before, and Zack saw no reason why it should not work this time.

It would be too obvious to use horses and carts, so a team of discreet, darkly-clothed men would carry the goods to the cliff bottom. Reuben would not be taking part. He would go to the pub, and keep an ear to the ground for any problems.

'Alreet, Reub. That's t'last o't fish,' said Zack, as the last barrels were loaded onto his cart.

'Good luck,' he whispered, as Silas cast off the mooring rope and he and Sandy took to the oars and gently manoeuvred the boat back out into deep water. Zack raised the sails, and once clear of the tide race, changed course until he could come about

159

and glide into the anchorage below the cliffs. As the tide receded, the boat would ground on the firm sand, and settle on her side, allowing the crew to jump overboard and walk home. Big Isaac had kept a low profile during the landing of the fish, so no-one saw that he had been left on board as watch-keeper.

Silas and Sandy jumped agilely onto the beach, and Zack followed more slowly. To any watching 'sniv', this was the normal thing to be doing. The three men shouldered their gear and walked to the slipway, then loudly said their farewells and returned to their own homes.

It was a long and anxious wait until it was dark enough for Silas to lead his team of six strong men back to the waiting *Elizabeth*. Two by two they wandered nonchalantly down to the slipway. They paused a moment by the wall of the inn which occupied the corner close to the shore. All clear. No lights on in the watch house only a few feet away from them. Sandy and his partner were first away, followed a few minutes later by Silas and the other four.

It was not a long walk out to the boat, but in the dark it was easy enough to stumble on an unseen rock or slip on a treacherous strand of seaweed.

Meanwhile, up on the cliff top, Zack had organised his team. They had met in the Mariners Tavern, which was most handily situated with its rear entrance leading off the narrow track which ran close behind the cliff edge buildings. The front door, by which most of the customers entered, opened straight into the bar. This was the very same door that had been watched so closely, many years ago, by the village constable Jos Clarke, who with Peter Maxwell and James Herbert had spent a freezingly cold night waiting to capture the notorious David Pinkney. Zack smiled at the recollection of that eventful night, which had been the talk of the village for weeks. Pinkney had got away, so the constable had lost face and experienced considerable embarrassment in consequence.

There was a small garden behind the inn, with tough salt-tolerant bushes providing protection from the blasting sea winds. Tonight, these not only provided shelter for the building, but also for the half dozen men, led by Zack, who crouched low, awaiting a sign from below.

A strong wind had blown up, and although the noise from the waves breaking over the distant rocks would help disguise any faint sounds such as thuds from barrels knocking against the cliff, no-one dared speak or shout. A long rope with a strong net bag at the end had been suspended over the edge at the agreed spot, and as soon as the first of the kegs had been carried from the *Elizabeth* and attached to the rope, a violent tug would announce the time had come to begin hauling.

Zack waited until he felt the signal, then beckoning to the rest of his team, they paired up and dropped two more ropes over the edge. Carefully, slowly, hand over hand, the ropes were hauled up, and the kegs appeared. Pairs of waiting hands carried them to the rear entrance of the Mariners, where Thomas Knaggs the innkeeper was waiting to store them in his cellar.

Zack was sweating with anxiety, as four dozen kegs would take a lot of handling. It said a lot for the reliability and experience of his team that by the time the fortieth keg had been settled into its temporary home, he began to breathe more easily. Towards the end of such a successful 'run', the relief was enormous.

Finally, the vigorous double tug from below signalled that the keg now on the rope's end was the very last. Up it came, and as it disappeared into the tavern's cellar, the teams pulled up the ropes, coiled and tied them neatly around their waists, tugged their ganseys into shape, and silently dispersed to their homes.

All that remained to do was gradually, over the next few weeks, to transport the brandy to the home of the squire. Now that the landing was safely accomplished, they could take their time over that. No point in rushing it. Wait until any suspicion had completely gone, then no one would suspect the cart which normally delivered the weekly order of fish and vegetables to Thorpe Hall carried a little extra special cargo!

Big Isaac was skilful at carpentry, and installed an ingenious box seat in the rear of Reuben's cart. He, along with Damaris and Ben became a familiar sight on the narrow lanes, as they delivered fish to neighbouring farmsteads. The space under the seat was craftily accessed from underneath the cart, and no amount of poking and prying revealed any hinged panels, as the floorboards were cunningly devised to slot into place from below.

On the days that the fish was delivered to Thorpe Hall, a little extra 'something' was also securely on board. Damaris knew about the contents under the seat, but Ben was always sent away to play happily with the kittens or into the kitchen to cadge some cake from the cook whilst the goods were unloaded. He enjoyed the trips out, and his presence on the cart lent an air of innocence, but it was still wiser and safer for him not to know, in case he started asking awkward questions. He was growing into a very inquisitive child.

The six men who had been the landing team took it in turns to drive the cart, and each had a different day and took a different route, so there was no chance of a clear routine being discovered. These men were the only ones in the village who knew about the squire's brandy, and all were one hundred percent trustworthy. At the end of each successful delivery, a few significant winks and nods were exchanged, but that was all.

All went well until the very final delivery was due. It was Silas' turn to drive the cart, and he set off in cheerful good spirits. It would be such a relief when it was all over, and from tomorrow they could really regard the *Elizabeth* as their own. They would owe the squire nothing. From now on, things would really be looking up.

Silas made the deliveries to the farms, then turned the cart and, whistling merrily, confidently drove through the watersplash that forded the stream which ran alongside the gardens of Thorpe Hall, then turned sharp right into the driveway. He drove round to the back, and reversed the cart close to the rear doorway.

Whilst the servants unloaded the fish, Silas ducked underneath the cart and withdrew the sliding floorboards. Carefully lowering the final two kegs of spirits, he rolled them into the kitchen, replaced the boards, and jumped back in the driving seat.

Now that it was all done, he had a slight and unexplained feeling of unease. He had suspected that he had been watched as he turned into the Hall driveway, but shrugged away the thought as nervous foolishness. He shook the reins and clicked at the horse to get moving. He would be glad to get home.

Just clear of the entrance gates, a uniformed figure stepped in front of him. 'Halt, in the name of the King!' demanded an imperious voice. Silas' heart beat fast in his chest, but he drew a calming breath and drew the horse to a stop.

'Get down from there,' said the man in a tone of voice not to be argued with. 'Where have you been?'

'Just deliverin' the fish, as Ah allus do,' replied Silas calmly.

'I believe you have more than fish in that cart. Stand aside and let me look.' The wretched man clearly meant business. Horatio Roberts, newly appointed chief of the King's Waterguard, and a man full of his own self-importance, roughly pushed Silas aside. Silas was not overduly worried, as he had, fortunately unloaded the kegs, and had replaced the floorboards with the utmost care. All that was left in the cart was a single box of herring, which, under the strengthening sun was beginning to smell.

The horse began to get restless, and chomped on the bit. He danced a little from side to side, and then, getting the bit between his teeth, took off down the lane, the cart leaping and bumping behind him. The more the cart bumped, the more agitated the horse became, and Silas started to run to catch him.

'Stop!' bawled Horatio Roberts in stentorian tones, but neither horse nor a frantic Silas took any notice. 'Stop!' he bawled even louder, 'or I fire!'

Silas could not stop, even if he had wanted to, as his hands were twisted in the reins, and the horse was dragging him along.

'Whoa!' he shouted, but the panicking horse took no notice, and careered along the narrow lane.

Suddenly there was a tremendous 'bang!' and Silas felt an excruciating pain in his leg. He let go of the reins and fell, bleeding heavily, in the road. The horse had already gone on without him.

The evidence had run away. Roberts had no proof, and losing face was not on his agenda, so he replaced his pistol in its holster, leant against the gatepost, and watched whilst Silas dragged himself to the side of the road, and eventually rose painfully and limped towards home. The officer looked back thoughtfully at the beautiful residence of the squire. He was pretty sure his hunch had been right, but what chance was there of arresting the squire for being in possession of contraband? He was, after all, the chief of the local magistrates.

# - 12 -

The door of the Storms' cottage opened without warning, and in walked a tall, smart young man in the uniform of a Royal Naval midshipman. A kit-bag hung from his shoulder. He carried his hat under his arm, and his hair was short and neatly brushed. His brass buttons gleamed and twinkled in the sunlight.

Liz looked up from her baking and stared with undisguised admiration and astonishment, for it was a moment or two before she actually acknowledged that this unrecognised young man, standing silhouetted in her doorway, was her formerly rebellious and slovenly son.

He stepped forward smartly, and dumped his hat and his kit-bag on the kitchen table.

'Matthew!' she shouted delightedly, and ran to embrace him, briefly wiping her hands on her apron as she did so. Matt, smiling, put out his hands to deter her.

'Let me tek me jacket off, Ma... Ah dean't want it all floury!' He swiftly shrugged himself out of the precious garment, then held out his arms for the delayed hug.

'Tha can wash me shirt - it don't matter aboot that gettin' mucky!'

She held him at arms length, a broad grin on both their faces as she held her head on one side and surveyed him critically. Had he been fed well enough? She'd heard a lot about bad navy food, but, she had to admit - reluctantly if truth were told - that he looked extraordinarily fit and well. He'd grown taller, of course, but had also filled out with broad shoulders and a firm chest. My, he was handsome! The local girls would be flocking round him like bees to a honey pot. Well now, this was a lovely surprise. Liz was used to her menfolk coming and going without much announcement, but this really was an unexpected treat. Occasionally letters got through on the regular mail coach to Whitby, but obviously Matthew had docked in Newcastle and caught the very first coach home.

Wait until Zack came in! He'd be that proud of his son. Liz was delighted when Matt explained that he would be at home for a couple of months whilst *Pelican* was in dock for a re-fit, if she could put up with him cluttering up her kitchen, he teased. They would be a family again, just as in the old days - but Liz corrected that, for this new Matthew was so different from the surly and difficult teenager she had so lost patience with. For sure, this was going to be a very happy time.

Matt was anxious to go and see Reuben, and thank him for all his help. He also had much news from Reub's old mates aboard the *Pelican*, and a message from Captain Searle. He wanted to rush round and see Captain Emerson, and tell him all that he had been doing, how he was now studying for his lieutenant's ticket, and that he had found several officers on board who would willingly help him with his studies.

The old sea-dog's eyes misted with pride, as he saw what a fine young man Matthew had become. If he had had a son, thought Captain Emerson, and he had turned out like Matthew, he would have been well pleased. Young Storm would be a credit to his family, his village, and the King to whom he had sworn allegiance when he took the traditional King's Shilling.

Silas dragged himself to the side of the road and collapsed onto the grass verge. He felt faint as a cold sweat broke out on his forehead. Putting his head between his knees and taking deep, calming breaths of air, he gradually felt the world was not swimming round him. Carefully removing his left boot and rolling up his trouser leg he surveyed the damage of the gunshot wound. It was still bleeding heavily, and he gingerly felt round the back of the calf to see if he could find an exit hole for the bullet. He could not, but he could feel a solid lump lodged against his shin bone.

Damn and blast, the bullet was still in there. He would have been much happier if the bullet had gone right through his leg, for all he would have had to do was to make sure the wound was cleansed and well bound up. The healing process would take time, but it should heal without too much problem. With the bullet still lodged in his leg, however, this was a much more serious matter. Unless it was dealt with, the wound could go gangrenous, and he might even lose his leg. Silas tried not to panic.

He tore a strip off the cleanest part of his shirt, bound the bleeding leg tightly, then painfully dragged himself to his feet and started the long limp home. He could not believe his luck when, as he rounded the corner, there was the horse, still attached to the cart, harness hanging loose, and contentedly munching mouthfuls of the lush grass that grew along the roadside.

Quietly and calmly he approached, making reassuring sounds. The horse looked up briefly, then went on munching. Silas gently took hold of the harness and readjusted the bridle and bit, then agonizingly hauled himself up into the driving seat. The effort brought on another wave of fainting, but after a while of resting, he shook the reins over the horse's back, and encouraged him into a slow and easy walk. Silas had never been so glad to see a horse in his life, and even gladder when he eventually drew up alongside the stable to see Big Isaac waiting for him.

'Bye, lad. Tha's tekken thi tahm! Wheer hast tha bin?' he enquired. For a reply, Silas slumped down in the seat again, pointing to his leg and the pool of blood which was now congealing on the floor of the cart.

Isaac gently lifted Silas to the ground and laid him on a pile of sacking. He scratched his head and wondered what on earth they should do. Silas needed treatment, and quickly before the shock of the injury wore off and real pain set in.

All he could think of was where could he find a doctor who could be trusted to operate, and not ask questions. He knew that even if they covered Silas' face while the operation was carried out, enquiries would still soon follow, and once the 'snivs' had got their teeth into this, they'd be like Yorkshire terriers, and not let go. Then, after all the hard work and secrecy, the news of their last haul would be out, and not even the squire could - or would - save them.

From what Silas had managed to gasp out to Isaac regarding the incident, he was almost confident that Horatio Roberts would not be saying anything. He'd lost face by not having any proof, and he'd certainly not get anywhere by investigating the squire.

'Lay there, lad,' said Isaac gently, smoothing Silas' hair back from his brow. 'Ah'll gan and fetch Zack. He'll knaw what ti deah. Stay still, and rest.'

Silas managed a weak smile. 'Ah'm not likely ti be ganin far wi this, am Ah?'

'Ah'll not be long,' said Isaac as he shut the stable door, and headed off to find Zack.

168

Zack was just finishing his dinner, and enjoying listening to Matthew's tales of life in the navy. The lad seemed to be doing well, and Zack was incredibly proud of him. All the waiting and frustration now seemed worth it.

Isaac knocked on the door and peered round it before being invited in. He was trying to control the panic which was setting in. Normally, Isaac was a bit slow of thought and movement, and bumbled about like a big clumsy carthorse, but today Zack straight away saw that something was amiss. His immediate thought was that Silas had been intercepted on his last delivery, but Isaac was able to reassure him on that count. However, the news about Silas' injury was not good, and Matthew listened attentively.

After a while, when Zack and Isaac had discussed the difficulty of finding a trustworthy doctor, Matthew stood up and put his hand on Isaac's arm. 'Would tha let me hev a leuk at him?' he enquired, looking across at Zack. 'Ah'm nay surgeon meself, but Ah hev acted as loblolly boy to t'surgeon on t'*Pelican*. Ah've helped wi' a lot of bad injuries, and even helped amputate, though Ah sincerely hope Ah won't have to do that ti poor owd Silas.' Matt shuddered at the gory memories of bloody and pain-filled moments on the orlop deck. 'Ah can at least hev a leuk and see how bad he is. Then we'll see what we have to do.'

Matt went into the kitchen and rummaged about until he had found a sharp skewer and a couple of small knives, a candle and a tinder box. He wrapped the instruments in a clean cloth, and told Zack to go down into the cellar and decant a fair amount of brandy into smaller bottles which he could hide in his jacket pocket. He'd need that both for cleansing the wound, and also for drugging Silas while he operated. By the time they got back to the stable, the first searing pain would have dulled, making the new probing much more painful. Matt bundled up clean cloths for bandages, and a pad to put in Silas' mouth as a gag for him to bite on.

When all was ready, the three men left the cottage in as casual a way as possible under the circumstances, and Isaac led them to the stable.

Silas was conscious, but in great pain. Matthew took his hand and explained what he would have to do. 'Let me have a look,' he said gently, and turned Silas' leg so he could see the entry point of the bullet. Carefully probing with his fingers, he felt the hard lump of lead resting against Silas' shin bone. Matthew hoped that the bone was not splintered, otherwise they would be in real trouble.

He did not voice this thought, but said to Silas, 'Ah think we're alright theer. Bullet's not too deep in, but it'll still hurt. Have a good strong swig of this whilst Ah'm getting thee cleaned up.' Silas grimaced as the neat brandy burned his throat. He was not used to so much neat strong spirit, which was a good thing, as it numbed his senses a good deal quicker. 'Reet, anither swig!' He watched as Silas struggled to aim the bottle at his mouth.

'Ah think he's gettin' dopey,' said Matthew. 'Now Isaac, stand oot o' me light, and keep watch outside t'door. Light up thi pipe, and lean up on t'wall as if tha's hevin a little rest from work. Zack, be ready ti hand me tools as Ah ask. And dinna faint on me,' he said with a slight smile. Zack was affronted, but said nothing. He was not looking forward to this.

Matthew put into practice the tidy habits of the ship's surgeon, as he laid out the instruments on the clean cloth. Lighting the candle with the tinderbox, he quickly passed the skewer and the knife blades through the flames to sterilise them then soaked a clean rag in the brandy and wiped away any vestige of soot.

170

'Now Zack, put this pad across his mouth and let him bite on it. We can't let 'im scream. Hold his leg tight, Ah need 'im ti keep very still.'

Matthew drew a deep breath and as gently and quickly as possible, took the smallest knife and made a clean incision. 'Skewer!' he said to Zack, just like the surgeon on the *Pelican* had called for his instruments. Matthew felt with the probe, following the angle he thought the bullet had entered. He sighed with relief. Got it first time. Carefully he opened the incision a little further and inserted the knife under the bullet. Silas struggled and screamed into his gag. Zack administered another strong swing of brandy, and Matthew rested until it had taken effect. With a deft flick of the knife, the bullet shot out onto the floor.

The wound was bleeding profusely, and Zack was a bit alarmed, but Matthew reassured him that was a good thing, as it would wash out any bits and infection. He let it bleed for a while, then wetted a clean rag, and cleaned up the cut. He poured brandy into the wound, then carefully bound the edges together with a clean bandage.

The blood still seeped through, but Matthew was not worried. Padding more bandages over and pulling them as tight as he dared, Matthew then asked Zack to raise Silas' leg to help stop the bleeding. They packed him up on a pile of sacking, and finally removed the gag.

Zack gave him another swig of the brandy, and a big smile, telling him it was now all over, and that although he would feel pain for some time, the wound would heal well. He hadn't lost his leg, but he would have an impressive scar to show the girls, smiled Matthew as he ruffled Silas' hair.

He stood back, proud at a job well done.

He was not, however, as proud as his father, who put an arm round his son's shoulders and gave him a manly hug. Only then did reality dawn on Matthew, as he said, 'Reet, then, how about a swig o' brandy fer t'surgeon! Ah reckons he needs one as much as t'patient!'

Silas rested on a soft pile of hay until the effects of the brandy began to wear off and he sobered up enough for him to be helped to his feet. Even Isaac became alarmed at the slurred singing Silas was serenading them with. After all the secrecy surrounding the operation, it would be the devil if t'owd chap gave t'game away with his singing.

Zack stood handy with the gag, just in case, and Isaac kept popping his head round the stable door to make sure Horatio Roberts wasn't on the prowl.

Zack ragged Silas, that if he'd had his leg off, he could have had a peg-leg, like one of the old sea Captains of his father's generation. That ancient worthy had hollowed out his wooden leg and filled the space with contraband tobacco, with which he blatantly limped ashore right under the noses of the Revenue men. None of them need ever be short of tobacco again!

Silas managed a hiccup and a grin. He'd prefer to keep his own leg, thank you very much.

## - 14 -

The weather had been frustratingly calm for several days. The boats gently rocked at anchor on the slight swell. There was not a breath of wind. Zack wetted his finger and held it up, but could feel nothing. Zack, Big Isaac, Sandy, Reuben and Matthew sat about with the other deep-sea fishermen, impatient to get off earning. It was infuriating, having spent so much effort and money in buying the big boat, only to be idling around with no income, watching the small coble-men busying about in the Bay, as they hauled in profitable catches of crabs and lobsters. Isaac looked across at the worried expressions of his fellow crew-mates. Had they really done the right thing?

Matthew had also wondered if his father had done the right thing. He had not been at home to be consulted. If he'd stayed home instead of being so determined to better himself in the navy, would the others have been forced into this decision? Had he really been expected to follow his father into the family boat, working in partnership with Reub, and allowing Zack to take the retirement for which he was long overdue? He would probably never know, and anyway, it was too late now, but seeds of worry had rooted themselves in Matt's mind.

He had temporarily taken Silas' place on the *Elizabeth*, and as he was on half pay from the navy whilst the *Pelican* was in dock, and was living at home with no additional expenses, he agreed to give Silas his share of the profits. Liz was happy with the idea, as she was just so delighted to have Matthew home again for a few weeks, especially since he was now so different to live with. Liz almost missed the surly teenager banging around moodily, but she was just so proud of the fine young man who had replaced him.

If he had stayed home, most likely he would have turned from a surly, rebellious teenager into an embittered man.

Silas was now back in the village, and explained his limp as being due to a bad fall from his horse. He came round to the Storms' cottage on a regular basis, for Matthew to keep an eye on the cleaning of the wound. Each time he removed the bandages, Matthew bent low over the leg and sniffed for any faint trace of gangrene. Evidently the bone had not splintered, and Matthew's careful cleaning had been successful. The healing process was going well, and the young 'doctor' was secretly proud of his efforts. Maybe, he thought, he would eventually become a ships' surgeon. It would, however, be a while before Silas was fit enough to go back full time fishing. They would have to find a temporary replacement once Matthew's leave was over, but for now things would do fine as they were.

Zack was quite thrilled to have Matthew back on the boat with himself and Reuben. It was almost like old times, except that now Matt was so much more mature, and it was a pleasure having him around. He had developed into a sensible and capable seaman, and Zack watched with admiration at the way the young man handled the boat. Zack was almost sorry that this would not be a permanent arrangement - father and son working together, as many of the other fishing families did. He understood, however, that things had changed and still were changing, and a future in the fishing industry was becoming increasingly uncertain. It would probably last for his lifetime, but he had noticed that some very elderly men were still struggling to go out to make a living. What would there be for Matthew's generation? Sandy remarked that it was all very well having this nice new big boat, but if they'd still had the old cobles they could have been off fishing today instead of hanging about waiting for the wind. He looked almost enviously at the small cobles busily at work close in to the Bay.

They needed the wind to sail right beyond the horizon. They could not row that far, and they also needed to be sure they would have enough wind to get back home again! That was one of the drawbacks of the deep-sea fishing, one that would not be solved in their lifetimes, until in the next century fishing boats would have engines which would not only make life safer, but more profitable as well, as larger catches would be brought home on a more frequent basis. But that was in the unknown future, and was no help to Zack and the crew of the *Elizabeth*.

Zack's stomach rumbled, indicating it was time for dinner, so he knocked out his pipe, and stretched his stiff legs and back. Reuben followed suit and headed off to home and Damaris, and Sandy left to have a bite and a pint of ale at the inn.

Only Isaac remained, deep in thought. His mind did not work as quickly as the others' but once he got an idea, nothing would let him rest until he had followed it through. His gaze rested on the distant horizon, and he began thinking about his long-dead father. He was one of the 'old school' and had hung on to many of the ancient superstitions and beliefs. He used to say that a fisherman could 'buy' a wind that would bring him safe home if becalmed. He had to take the wind with him, and only use it if he needed to. It was a dangerous thing to have, and had to be used with the greatest care. His old father said you could buy such a wind from a witch. The nearest thing they had to a witch round here was old Jennet...

Isaac wondered if she knew anything about it. There was only one way to find out. He did not relish the idea of walking all the way out to the odd little hut where she lived, and truth to tell he was a bit nervous of her peculiar looks and habits.

Isaac sat alone on the seat in his favourite spot and thought hard. Gradually he persuaded himself that this was one thing he could do to help in a practical way.

He wondered if anyone he knew had ever done this. He would probably never find out, as it was not something they would want to talk about, and neither would he, he decided. This was to be his secret. His, and Jennet's. After a while, some instinct told him if he was going to do this he must go now, so whilst the others were at their dinners, Isaac started on the long walk through Little Wood and across the fields to Jennet's cottage.

Isaac leant with his arms on the top bar of the gate which led to the field, in the far corner of which stood Jennet's tumbledown cottage. Long ago it had been a summer shelter for one of the shepherds, but for many years now it had been the isolated home of a strange and lonely old lady. No sheep grazed the luscious meadow, which seemed a shame. The whole atmosphere was one of complete desertion. The air was totally still and uncannily quiet. It was weird, and Isaac began to feel very uneasy.

The weather was hot and muggy for the time of year, and Isaac was a little out of breath after his long walk through the woods and across the fields. He removed his cap and mopped his forehead with his kerchief and looked around him nervously, in case he'd been followed. This whole business was making him uneasy, but having come this far, he'd better get on with it. He paused a while, thinking over what he should say. He was not good with words, and rehearsed his opening sentence over and over. When he was sure he'd got it right, he took a deep breath, opened the gate and started on the last part of his fateful journey.

A thin wisp of smoke rose from the chimney, so it looked as though she was at home. As he came close to the cottage, he leant on the gate. There was at first no sign of her, but after a while, his eyes focussed, and he could see Jennet bending over and gathering the herbs which grew in her garden.

She wore a long greyish green skirt and shawl which had blended perfectly with the herbs, which was why she had not been instantly visible. Beside her, as she worked, sat her one-eyed cat, desultorily washing itself in the sunshine. It paused for a moment and regarded him disdainfully, then totally ignoring his presence, continued its ablutions.

Isaac was relieved that he had met Jennet in the garden. Hopefully he would not then have to enter the cottage where he knew he would feel ill at ease and trapped. As the gate clicked shut behind him, Jennet straightened up and with a groan placed her hand in the small of her back, looking at him disconcertingly.

'Now then, Isaac,' she greeted him in the abrupt way Bay folk traditionally greeted each other. 'What's ti deah wi thee, then? What's thee wantin' of me?' She knew few people visited her socially. They always wanted something, whether it was medicine, advice or sometimes a love potion or even a curse. She looked at him keenly. He was too old to want a love potion, and he didn't look the kind to want a curse. It must be a medicine.

Isaac did not reply.

'Dost tha need summat fer a bad back?' she asked, trying to help him find the words. Backache was common amongst the fishermen.

Isaac removed his cap, and stood, twisting it in his hands in embarrassment. He shook his head. 'Or a cough?' she suggested helpfully. Isaac shook his head again and looked at the ground between his feet. He had trodden on a sprig of thyme, and the sweet aroma lingered on the warm air. It was a smell that would come back to haunt him for the rest of his life.

'Best come inside, then.' Isaac shrugged and indicated that he would rather talk in the garden, so Jennet went into the cottage and returned with a couple of rickety chairs. Big Isaac sat down gingerly; he felt the chair wobble under his weight, and that did not add to his confidence.

'Well, now. Is tha goin' ti tell me what tha's coom all this way fer?' Putting her head on one side, and looking at him lopsidedly, she commented, 'Ah doesn't suppose it's jest a social call, is it, Isaac?'

Isaac shook his head, then diffidently gathering courage, he told her all about the new boat, and how they had worked so hard to pay for it. Now it was all theirs, they needed to earn money for the long winter ahead. Zack, Reuben, Silas and Sandy had families dependent upon their earnings. Isaac, at least, had only himself to care about, and his needs were few and simple.

For the past week, he explained, they had been becalmed and unable to set out for the distant fishing grounds, and even if the wind did lift within the next few days, they still could not be sure that the weather would return to normal and there would be enough wind to fill their sails to get them home.

Isaac, having been all his life a small coble fisherman, had not yet accustomed himself to the new routine, and, although not admitting it, had a deep-set fear of not returning home. Without a favourable wind to help them, there was no way they could row themselves back into the Bay. He'd had nightmares about being marooned miles out to sea, with no one to rescue. On the worst nights of dreams, Isaac had seen himself, alone and the last man alive, gasping for fresh water. He would never admit his dreams to his mates, but deep down he realised that, unlikely though it seemed he, 'Big' Isaac, was afraid.

Settling himself down to continue with his strange request, Isaac told Jennet that he believed that a wise woman - he advisedly did not use the term 'witch' - could provide the answer. He was here to 'buy' a wind. He rummaged in his pocket, and held out his hand. Two gold coins lay shining in his palm.

Why, in the heat of the sun, did that gold turn to ice in his calloused hand? Isaac did not know why, but he shivered, and a cold sweat broke out on his forehead.

Jennet said doubtfully, yes, this was possible, but it was a dangerous thing to ask, and she was not sure she could, or should, do it. She carefully and slowly explained how the charm took effect, so that Isaac was absolutely sure he knew what he was asking her to do for him.

A length of knotted rope was endowed with the power of producing the required wind, and as each knot was untied, so the charm unloosed the wind. The user had to judge the untying very carefully, too many knots untied too quickly could easily bring on a storm. It really was a very risky business. She frankly believed that she should not do it.

Isaac's face showed such disappointment that Jennet said very well, she would try, but he must be completely sure he understood how to use it. He, and only he, must be the one to use it, and he must guard it with his life. 'Nivver, nivver let it out of thy sight. Understand?'

She got up and went into the cottage and after a while returned with a short length of thin rope. She sat back in her chair, threw her head back and closed her eyes. Isaac watched nervously as Jennet sank into the depths of a trance. Gradually her hands began to twitch, she rose to her feet, her eyes now wide open yet unseeing, and whirled the rope faster and faster round her head, all the while emitting a strange moaning sound. Isaac shuddered. It sounded just like a wind starting to blow.

The whirling stopped, and Jennet tied a knot in the rope. Then the whirling and moaning began again, and again she stopped and tied another knot. This was repeated the magical seven times, and finally Jennet sank back in the chair, her strange eyes staring right through and way beyond him. Then her eyelids drooped and she fell into a deep slumber. Isaac dared not move in case he woke her, and sat uneasily waiting until she came to.

Suddenly her eyes opened and she leapt from her chair with an alacrity that startled Isaac. She snatched clumsily at the two gold coins with her twisted hand, and threw the rope onto Isaac's lap.

'Go!' she commanded abruptly, and jerking to his feet, Isaac made to shake her hand. She turned away, repeating the single word, 'Go!'

Isaac coiled up the rope and put it in his pocket. He would not tell the others what he had done, and he hoped he would never have to use it.

Jennet stood stock still, watching until Isaac had lumbered across the field and through the far gate. She watched until he was right out of sight. Then she turned, exhausted, back to her cottage.

He could be carrying death in his pocket.

What had she done?

# - 16 -

The cat leaped onto Jennet's lap, waking her with a start, as its sharp claws penetrated her thin skirt. It arched its back and shivered its tail in the air as it trod round and round on her bony knees, trying to pad itself a comfortable hollow in which to settle down. With an instinctive animal empathy the cat seemed to sense that Jennet needed reassurance.

The dream from which she had been so suddenly wakened had been a disconcerting and troubling one. She had been floating high above the village, looking down onto what should have been a familiar sight, even from this strange new perspective, but it was all very new and unsettlingly strange.

There were none of the familiar fishing boats either on the sea or lying at anchor under the lee of the cliff. There were still a few small craft bobbing on the water, but they were not the ones she knew. None of them carried the brown tanned lug sails; some had small boxes with windows on the decks, and strange lumpy things hanging over the stern. The tide was out, and the shore was dotted with hundreds of brightly dressed figures. Looking more closely, Jennet could not recognise any of the people or their clothing. They were all strangers. The men wore some sort of coloured trousers which ended above the knee, and some of the women hardly had any clothes on at all. Jennet was horrified.

Plump children paddled at the edge of the sea, shrieking as the tiny waves washed over their feet. Some were digging in the sand, or running about shouting. She saw two familiar animals ambling along the beach, but instead of carrying baskets of nets and lines down to the boats, they were bearing children on their backs. What was going on? Where were the villagers she knew? She felt very alone.

At the bottom of the slipway which should have been crowded with the familiar boats, stood a strange sort of large white box with wheels at each corner. It was surrounded by excited children, all jostling each other to get to the front. From a hole in the side, a smiling man in a white coat leaned out with a handful of pale pointed shapes with blobs of pink or white balanced on the top. The youngsters grabbed these and licked at them with obvious enjoyment.

Hovering above the village itself, Jennet looked for familiar cottages from which she could take a bearing. The dull pantiled roofs which should have been softened with the moss and weathering of centuries glowed an almost garish red in the harsh sunlight. The sombre brown and green shades of paintwork had been replaced with bright and gaudy colours. The walls of some of the dull sandstone cottages were now white, cream, pink, green and yellow. They looked pretty, she thought, but these were not the homes of her friends. Colourful flowers cascaded from window boxes and baskets - very nice, but the hard-working fisherfolk did not have time or money to indulge in such fancies... Oh, well.

The tiny streets and alleyways were crowded with jostling people speaking strange languages. Jennet thought of the Tower of Babel she had read about long ago in her Bible. She looked for the familiar shops - the butchers, the bakers, the shoemakers; they had all gone. In their place, the shop windows displayed strange, useless objects with the name 'Robin Hood's Bay' emblazoned upon them.

The narrow street which led from the dock, where the boats should have been drawn up, to the path through Little Wood, was crowded with people standing outside one of the buildings. One by one they entered, and when they came out they were carrying small parcels wrapped in white paper. Some carried them back to the dock, where they sat on the edge of the pavement, opened their parcels, and began to eat hungrily. Whatever it was, she could not make out, but they seemed to be enjoying it.

From time to time, the crowds which flocked in the main street, pressed back to the sides to allow the passing of strange, noisy tin boxes full of people. Most of these came down as far as the slipway and then did a lot of complicated goings backwards and forwards before turning themselves round, causing a lot of commotion amongst the masses of people, before crawling back up the hill again. Some made loud honking noises, which annoyed the people standing in front of them, for they shook their fists and shouted. Jennet shook her head in amusement. What was the point of it all? She just did not understand at all. Where was the familiar village of her lifetime, and *where* were all the folk she knew?

The rough and muddy cobbled surface of the steep hill coming down into the village now looked smooth and black and shiny, and was edged with stripes of bright yellow. What on earth had they done that for? At the top of the hill were new streets, lined with large, smart, red brick villas. Who lived in those? They must be very rich indeed to live in such splendour.

Along the hillside towards the high cliffs of Ravenscar, where smoke should have been rising from the alum works, all was deserted, and the old workshops lay in tangled ruins. In their place ran a line of shiny parallel tracks. Moving slowly along them was a long, black snake with smoke puffing from its head, emitting dreadful grunting sounds, wheezing with effort, as she did herself when plagued with an asthma attack. The snake gave out an unearthly shriek. Lordy me, thought Jennet, what on earth is that?

As she watched, the snake started to vanish into a dark hole. She watched, fascinated, until the tail had disappeared. She was thankful when it had gone, and her world was quiet once more. She did not understand and she did not like it.

A strange feeling of faintness and light-headedness came upon her as time moved on once more. The shiny metal tracks and the big black snake had gone, and in their place was a rough grey path, along which people wearing very odd shaped things like basins on their heads, sat on most peculiar metal frames with two big wheels. By moving their legs up and down they made the contraptions move forwards. The riders were encased in shiny black stuff that clung to every curve of their bodies. It was most indecent.

It was all so unfamiliar that she became increasingly disturbed and distressed. Turning away from the colourful noise and confusion, she left the village rooftops, and floated away across the peaceful fields towards her own dear cottage. But try as she would, she could not find it.

It should be there, in the corner of that field, where it had been for centuries. She drifted back and forth in greater and greater agitation, which turned to blind panic. She could not find her home. Her herb garden had gone, though a few plants had self-seeded and grew in a straggly mass in the long grass. All she could see was a pile of jumbled stones in the place where it should have been.

A tangle of brambles scrambled over them, and she reached down to push them aside. The sharp thorns pricked her hands and knees, and she awoke with a start to feel the cat padding about on her lap.

Her heart was thumping and she was sweating with fear - but - she was back home!

## 17

Early on the Monday morning, Zack woke up to feel a steady breeze blowing. The curtains at their bedroom window wafted into the room. He turned to Liz and said, 'The wind's reet at last. We'll get off today. Ah'll get up and wake Matt, then he can fetch the others whilst Ah get t'rest o' t'gear tigether.'

The nets and lines had been aboard, ready for sailing, so all that remained was to fetch the bait from the store house, as they would attach the bait to the hooks as they were sailing out to the fishing grounds. Warm clothes waited, ready packed in the kit-bags, and Liz quickly completed the packages of food for the next few days.

Whilst Zack gathered the remaining gear, Liz put the kettle on the fire, and reached for the frying pan. Soon a wonderful smell of frying ham and eggs wafted through the kitchen. A loaf of new bread and a dish of glistening country butter lay on the table. She would ensure that Zack went away with a good meal inside him. She would eat this last meal with him, but knew she would not really taste it.

She loathed this new routine, knowing she would not see Zack until the end of the week. She missed his comforting presence in her bed, where the two of them fitted snugly together like nesting spoons. Weekday nights were lonely and chilly without him. Like the other women, however, Liz knew that this was the only way forward, since they could no longer make a regular income from the smuggling which, although dangerous, had given them a very comfortable standard of living for as long as she could remember - certainly for most of their married life. Now, with Zack in his late sixties, she felt aggrieved that he had to make such radical changes in their lifestyle simply to make ends meet.

She could not bear to stand with the other wives on the slipway and wave him off. He missed her presence there, and turned aside as the other men hugged the women goodbye. He understood, and treasured the thought of their own private farewell earlier that morning. He had an uneasy feeling it may have been their last...

'Reet, lads. Let t'women get back ti their chores - tha knaws they've got work ti deah, same as us. Tha can kiss 'em all tha likes coom Friday!' he remarked with a false cheerfulness. He, too, hated the moment of parting. The sooner the painful moment passed the better. And with that, the men made their way to the waiting boat.

There was much to do to get the *Elizabeth* afloat and moving, and as soon as Zack felt her keel lift and leave the safety of the sandy beach, the sails were up and filling with the gentle wind. Soon she was heading for the fishing grounds, her bows rising and falling proudly as she gathered speed.

The *Elizabeth* was a good boat, and in spite of being so much larger than the cobles he had sailed all his working life, she handled beautifully and sweetly - just like the woman she was named for.

Zack stood in the stern, his strong hands on the tiller, and looked back at the beloved village quickly shrinking into a miniature landscape behind him. He fixed the image in his mind, as he had a strong premonition that he would not see it again.

He shrugged away the thought before the others could see his expression and ask what was troubling him. There was work to do, and he had better put his mind to it.

## 18

Liz was even more unsettled than usual. She knew if she stayed in the house she would be tempted to look out of the window and watch her husband go, and be unable to call him back. A small voice nagged at the back of her mind. 'Come back! Come back!' it persisted.

She knew she needed to get out of the house until Zack was safely away. She needed some space. It was no good going to see old Isaac and Rebecca, as they would want to know all about their one remaining son. How was he? How was the new boat doing? Had he gone off this morning? When did she expect him back? How was Matthew? My, how proud they were of him! Had he got a girl yet? Was Damaris alright, and why hadn't Liz brought little Ben with her, she knew how Rebecca loved to see the boy and find him a few forbidden treats. The questions would be endless, and Liz knew she would soon feel exasperated, and lose patience with the garrulous old lady.

It was natural for Rebecca, especially, to want to chatter, as she now was unable to leave the house, and visitors were always a good source of news and village gossip. Liz understood, but did not want to speak about Zack just at the moment. Maybe she would go and visit the old couple later in the day when she felt calmer.

Instead, she would go and check on Jennet. The walk through the cool wood and across the field would be good for her state of mind. She would have some time to herself. Liz shook the shawl from her head, and tied it round her waist. Her long hair blew free in the wind, and she ran her fingers through it, feeling it lift in the cooling breeze.

Golden autumn sunshine dappled through the trees, highlighting the brilliant green of the ferns which grew so prolifically in the damp atmosphere. Soft mosses coated the tree barks, the distinctive odour of fungus tainted the air. Ahead of her, an opportunist squirrel poised, paws raised, enquiring head on one side, watching her cautiously with beady black eyes. It had not time to stay, for autumn was swiftly coming and it had urgent work to do. With a flick of its bushy tail it was off through the trees on its search for the hazelnuts which grew here in abundance.

Once through the wood, Liz climbed the stile and sat for a moment on the top rail, looking back the way she had come, then, swinging her legs over, climbed into the field towards the gate where the cattle always gathered. In winter they churned the mud into a quagmire, but in summer the clay dried into hard, sharp ridges. Whatever the season it was never easy to cross.

The cows jostled and shoved as Liz carefully opened the gate and squeezed through. Slapping the nearest on the rump, she pushed her way through the milling herd, picked her way carefully over the hard ridges of ground and set off across the field towards the cottage.

The garden gate was closed, and no smoke arose from the twisted chimney. That was unusual, for Jennet always had a fire, even in the heat of summer. Liz lifted the latch, the gate squeaked on its hinges and the sound seemed unnaturally loud in the still silence of the morning. The sun was now high in the sky, and gave off enough warmth to waft the familiar fragrant smell from the herbs spilling untidily across the path.

A few late flowering shrubs straggled against the hedge. It all needed a good tidying up, she thought. Matthew's care was missing, now that he was away so much. She'd have to see if he had an hour or two to come up and tame this horticultural jungle, which in her younger and fitter days had been Jennet's pride.

The cottage was uncannily quiet as Liz knocked on the shabby door. There was no sound from within. The cat lay on the doorstep, uncaring as Liz gently pushed it with her foot so she could open the door. The cat rose reluctantly, arched its back, yawned, stretched one hind leg and then the other, twitched its tail and nonchalantly stalked off down the path. It sat down a little way from her, curled its tail neatly over its paws and regarded Liz with a supercilious expression in its single eye, resenting being disturbed.

Liz shuddered - she recalled the unwelcome presence of the animal in her clean kitchen during the several weeks that Jennet - and the cat - had lived with her and Zack during Jennet's recuperation following her stroke. Liz did not particularly like cats anyway, and this one had settled itself in her kitchen, making itself so at home that Liz had wondered who really was boss in her own house. It had spat and scratched when she had ousted it from her fireside - *her* fireside, she reminded herself. Cats had that peculiar gift of making one feel inferior. No, she was *not* keen on that cat!

Liz listened again, her ear close to the door. Inside she could hear a faint scrabbling noise. It sounded like something rushing frantically backwards and forwards trying to get out. Calling out, 'Hello, Jennet. It's Liz. Can I come in?' and hearing no reply, Liz slowly opened the door.

She recoiled in alarm as a white hare shot past her into the garden, brushing her legs with its grubby fur. Liz, heart beating with fright, looked around the partly opened door, and nervously entered the dim and dusty room. In the corner, in her accustomed chair, sat Jennet. Her greeny-gold eyes were wide open, staring lifelessly ahead of her. She was quite dead.

Putting her hands over her face, Liz leaned against the doorway. She knew she should close those unseeing eyes, but could not bring herself to touch the body.

Quietly she closed the door and went back out into the garden. She felt quite sick with the shock of what she had found. The cat was nowhere to be seen, but the hare sat by the gate, watching and waiting. It raised its paw, almost in a gesture of farewell, loped through the open gate and into the wide fields beyond. Liz watched it for a while, as it crossed the grass and finally disappeared into a thicket of bushes.

It had gone and Jennet was finally free.

With a shock, Liz recalled the old superstition that it was bad luck for a fisherman to meet with a hare or certain other specific animals on the morning he was going to sea. In some fishing villages he would even return home and wait for another day. Liz knew that Zack had not seen the hare himself, but she had, and maybe that was a bad omen.

She must act quickly. She turned and raced back to the village to warn him, tripping on the long grass in her panic to get back in time. Her long skirts hampered her running, so she hitched them above her waist, not caring if she met anyone on the way. Her dark hair streamed behind her, and her shawl fell to the ground unheeded.

As she approached the cliff top which gave her a clear view of the wide Bay, she flopped down on the ground exhausted. She knew she was too late.

The *Elizabeth*, in full sail, was heading swiftly to the horizon.

## 19

The fishing went well, the weather was kind, and Neptune had been generous. Zack smiled to himself as he remembered the old tradition that his father and grandfather had told him about, and which he himself performed from time to time. He would cut a slice out of one of the cork floats of his nets and insert a coin. That ensured that Neptune knew that the fisherman had paid the great sea god for his munificence.

The payment had been accepted this week. The boxes and barrels were neatly packed as the two working cobles brought their catches alongside. The five men worked with a will and felt satisfaction and contentment. This was a good boat, and they knew they would soon have enough money to see them through the winter - as long as conditions remained like this.

Next season they may even be able to consider employing an extra man and a boy, as some of the more established boats did. Sometimes these extra men came out to sea, sharing the load, or were employed on shore, mending gear and delivering the catches. It was a true mark of success to become such an employer. It would also take some of the heavy work off Zack.

The sea remained calm, and conditions on board the *Elizabeth* were reasonably comfortable. The day's work was over, and the men were relaxing on deck. The two cobles were tethered to the mother ship, and gently bumped against the side in the swell. Zack commented to Mat he'd have to make a couple of rope fenders, otherwise some damage would be done.

The evening was calm, and the *Elizabeth* rocked gently at anchor. The bright moonlight shimmered on the dark water. It was a beautiful sight.

Over supper and a comforting pipe or two of tobacco, Sandy and Zack chatted over the old smuggling days, reminiscing as the elderly are wont to do. Reuben whittled at a piece of wood, making a whistle for little Ben. Matt was pottering about, tidying up the gear ready for turning for home when dawn broke next morning.

Isaac was asleep and comfortably snoring, so did not see when Matt picked up a length of rope with seven knots in it, which lay under the seat where Isaac dozed. Matt picked it up, and looked at it for a moment.

Bored now, with nothing to do, he idly untied the knots one by one. With it he could practise some of the fancy loops and hitches he was learning. He started to weave the intricate plait of a Turks head, but the rope was not long enough. It was tricky getting the first twists just right, otherwise the second and third weavings would not follow. It needed a fair bit of practice. Matt couldn't get it right, and finally lost patience.

Isaac gave a stentorian snore and woke himself up just in time to see Matthew, with a gesture of irritation, whirl the rope round his head and hurl it overboard.

'No!' he shouted and reached out his arms instinctively, falling to his knees in the bottom of the boat, but he was too late.

Matthew gave him a puzzled and enquiring look, and shrugged his shoulders. What was all that about? But Isaac only shook his head and slumped back on his seat, shuddering violently, head in hands.

The rope snaked away out of reach, hit the water with a splash, and slowly began to sink, leaving a trail of phosphorescent bubbles which glowed eerily as it sank out of sight.

Isaac imagined he saw a pale ghostly hand reach up and grasp it. The arm was clad in a navy blue fisherman's gansey.

## 20

A stealthy catspaw of wind ruffled the water and passed swiftly across the boat, causing Matt to look up anxiously at the sky. He did not like what he saw. Dark clouds were gathering on the horizon and moving rapidly towards them.

The surface of the sea turned to iron grey and the air chilled as the wind whipped up the waves and threw salt spray in their faces. Zack shivered and reached for his pea-jacket, shrugging himself into it and buttoning it up to the neck. He was getting too old for this sort of life, he thought, if he was feeling this cold. It occurred to him that it was not only the physical cold that was bothering him. Somehow he was beginning to feel fear. He had never been so apprehensive before, and when he saw how the waves were mounting up as the storm approached, for the first time in his life he had to admit he was feeling frightened. An icy hand seemed to grip at the pit of his stomach, and his hands began to shake.

They were a very long way from home.

Zack thrust his hands deep into the pockets of his pea-jacket, so that the others would not detect their trembling. He must not let the others sense his mounting panic. He looked anxiously across at Sandy and Isaac, and to Reuben and Matthew for reassurance, but there was none. He could see that they were as worried as he was. They had never experienced a storm of this intensity when they worked close to home in their old coble, and they were uncertain how to handle it. The *Elizabeth* felt very small and vulnerable, as she began tossing on the mounting waves. The sky was as dark as night, as a curtain of sleet swept rapidly across the face of the water.

In no time at all it was upon them.

The angry wind ripped at the flying black clouds, tearing them into ragged strips and flinging the sleet and spray hard into their faces. The waves built up into peaks of a frightening size, plunging them haphazardly down into the deep troughs. Each time, the *Elizabeth* shuddered as she thrust her bows upwards. She was fighting bravely. She was a good boat, well built, but was no match for the anger the storm was unleashing on them. Water surged in over the gunwales, and Sandy reached desperately for the baling can. It was hopeless, for gallons of sea water were now pouring into the boat, and she was beginning to settle under the extra weight. Soon she would be wallowing helplessly. Sandy tried to keep calm, for if panic set in, that would be fatal for all of them.

Behind them, Matt could see a huge wave dangerously rushing towards them, a sheer sheet of grey water which would surely swamp them over the stern unless they could somehow swing the boat round to meet it head on.

Matt had never experienced a storm of this ferocity in a small boat. He had, of course, been in a lot of rough weather in the North Sea, but that had been aboard the large and sturdy *Pelican*. This was a very different situation. His shouts of warning were borne away by the roaring of the wind, so instinctively, single-handed he threw his full strength on the tiller. The storm bore down relentlessly. They were a tiny vulnerable human speck on the turbulent seas.

The boat lurched and slewed, and before Reuben could realise what was happening and scramble to assist, the wave caught them broadside on, and the boat was thrown contemptuously over like a piece of driftwood. The passing wave roared on, chuckling at its destruction. In the icy water, five men struggled for their lives.

Normally they would not have worn their high sea boots, but for once in his life, uncharacteristically, Zack had sacrificed common sense and tradition to the biting cold, and this was his undoing, for as he sank, the boots filled with water and dragged him down.

Desperately he tried to kick them free and haul himself to the surface, but the waterlogged boots clung even more tenaciously, the thick cloth of the pea-jacket absorbed the water, and he could struggle no more. Gradually Zack lost his grip on life and fell into black unconsciousness.

Reuben and Matt struggled to the surface, and grasped the upturned hull of the boat. With a tremendous effort, they hauled themselves up until they could get a hold on the keel. Exhausted, they lay for a few moments, then shaking the streaming water from their hair and faces, they desperately searched for the others.

Matt shouted in panic as Reub took off his gansey and short boots and dived under the upturned boat to see if anyone was trapped underneath.

'Reub! Dinna leave me!' he yelled, and tears streamed down his face as his friend disappeared into the angry sea. He sat on the upturned hull, his mind a stunned emptiness. The few minutes that Reub was searching under the boat seemed for ever, and by the time he re-emerged, panting and shivering, Matt was realising the full enormity of his action.

Slowly and painfully Reub clambered back up and took a firm grip of the keel. Hauling himself breathlessly onto the upturned hull, he told Matt that there was no sign of the others. He wrung out his soaking gansey and struggled to pull it back on. He read Matt's mind, and tried to comfort him by saying he'd done absolutely the right thing - unfortunately, he was just that bit too late to save them, and the unpredictable sea had got the better of them. They both knew this could happen, but it always seemed to happen to somebody else.

Sandy and Isaac had been his crew mates, but they were of a different generation, and Matt did not know them that well, but Zack was his father, and when the realisation that his actions might have caused his father's death fully dawned upon him, Matt threw himself on Reub's shoulder and sobbed inconsolably with remorse. Reub realised the lad was suffering from severe shock, otherwise the gruff young man would never have given in to his emotions like this, even to Reuben.

There was still no sign of the others, even though Reub and Matt had shouted until they were hoarse. All they could do was to huddle together and wait for the sea to abate, and hope that the air trapped under the hull would give them buoyancy until daylight came and with it, perhaps - just perhaps - a chance of rescue.

Reub had not previously shared any of his naval experiences with Matthew. He had felt doing so would only rub up the young man's aggression. But now, with all that behind him, and his own naval career beginning, Matt's attitude had changed.

Now was the time to begin. Reub had to bring some distraction to the distraught young man huddling miserably beside him. There was nothing more either of them could do until the dawn broke.

So, on the dark and lonely sea, the two men shuffled on the upturned keel until they sat companionably back to back, each taking warmth and comfort from the other, and Reub once again told the story of the storm when they were nearly wrecked on the Isle of Jersey. That had been a terrifying night, but nothing half as bad as this one.

196

## 21

Sandy had been thrown clear of the capsized boat, and cast away on the departing wave. He was swept along for some distance until the wave lost its momentum, when it tired of playing with him, and left him behind, bobbing like a cork. Tossing the wet hair from his eyes, he dog-paddled to keep himself afloat. Now that he was alone in the water, his priority was to stay alive. The moon had come out again now that the storm had passed over, and his eyes became accustomed to the faint light which now glimmered spasmodically on the water.

A little way from him, he saw a drifting oar. Knowing that would help him keep afloat, he purposefully began to swim towards it. Reaching it, and tucking it under his arm, he rested and took stock of the situation.

There was no sign of the *Elizabeth*, but he could see, some distance away, what looked very much like one of her small attendant cobles. Mercifully, the coble was the right way up and still afloat.

Keeping the oar under his arm, Sandy began to swim strongly with his legs. With a bit of luck there might still be a second oar in the coble, but if not, Sandy knew that he could keep her head into the wind by using the single oar over the stern.

It seemed that as soon as he almost reached the floating coble, another wave came and swept it just out of his grasp. It was infuriating and exhausting, but Sandy persisted, and eventually held the side and dragged himself on board. With a huge sense of relief he collapsed on the deck-boards, closed his eyes, and slept.

He awoke to a lightening sky, and a faint moaning sound coming from under the sail which had collapsed when the wind had snapped the mast. Wonder of wonders, he was not alone.

Sandy scrambled to his knees and crawled towards the sound. He had no idea who his ship-mate was. He'd hoped beyond hope that it was Zack, whom he had last seen struggling helplessly in the water. Straining to lift the heavy waterlogged sail, he saw that it was not Zack, but Isaac. He had been knocked senseless by the falling mast and miraculously thrown into the coble instead of into the sea. He was bleeding heavily from a head wound, and moaning.

'Now then, Isaac,' Sandy gave him the traditional, curt Bay greeting. 'What's tha bin doin' ti thisen?' he asked the unconscious man, not expecting a reply. It was just comforting to use his voice in the presence of another human being. Shifting the sail and dragging the remains of the broken mast off Isaac's legs, Sandy made him as comfortable as possible and bound up his wound.

There was no food on board the small vessel, so they settled down to a long and hungry vigil, but at least they were both alive, though Isaac was drifting in and out of consciousness, muttering incomprehensibly during the short moments he came to.

The second oar was still in the bottom of the coble, trapped under Isaac's heavy body. Sandy pushed him aside, extricated the oar, and fitted both into the rowlocks. The small coble tended to bob about and slew round broadside unto the waves, corkscrewing sickeningly. Leaning exhausted on the oars, Sandy struggled to keep the small craft head on and steady. They'd had enough capsizing for one night.

Isaac still lay in the bottom of the boat. In the morning he would rag him for being such poor company. Meanwhile, Sandy worried about what had happened to the others. It was still too dark to see very far. All he could do was wait for the dawn and hope that there was someone else out there on the lonely ocean.

# - 22 -

The storm had passed as quickly as it had arisen. The curtain of sleet drew itself over them and away. The whipping spray eased, and the waves calmed into an uncanny quietness. As good a boat as the *Elizabeth* was, she had been no match for the unleashed forces of nature. This had not been a normal storm. The speed with which it had passed left them as the playthings of a primeval sea-god to be tossed and teased as a cat plays with a mouse.

Now that the noise of the wind had abated, there was a chilling silence on the desolate ocean. They were totally alone. It was pitch dark, for the passing storm had obliterated even the faint light a few distant stars would have shed. There was no moon. The sense of isolation was terrifying. They had no idea of the time - they could be drifting like this for hours. What if the storm should return? Reub had never known fear like this, and Matt told himself he should not be here... he was on leave, and was only in this situation because of Silas' injury. 'Bugger bloody Silas, and his bloody leg,' he muttered to himself as he miserably shrugged deeper into his wet gansey. 'And all because of the damned squire and his brandy!'

Reub began to explain to Matt how the only way they could get the money to pay the boat-builder was to borrow the residue from the squire. They had all raised as much as they possibly could, but it was nowhere near enough. Perhaps it *was* an over-ambitious project, but it seemed a good idea at the time, and anyway, it was far too late to be having doubts now. All was lost, but the price still had to be paid and it now looked as though it was all for nothing. Maybe the hull of the *Elizabeth* could be towed back to the village and repaired and re-fitted, but would any of them have the heart to start all over again?

Reub told Matt how nervous he had been when he had to be the one to go and ask, what a lot depended on him getting a favourable answer, and how the squire had made the stocking of his brandy cellar a condition of the loan. He started to wish he had never gone; had never had the grand idea that they could have a boat like the *Elizabeth* which should have brought them all good fortune. If it hadn't been for him, they would not be here now... He ignored the fact that it had been a joint decision, still taking the brunt of the blame on himself.

Reub thought back to the night he had told Ben about the storm which had nearly wrecked the *Pelican*, and related to Matt how he had taken the little lad out and stood with him on the balcony of the watch-house so that the child had some small idea of what his father had endured that night. He vowed he would never tell Ben and Damaris how afraid he was now... if he ever got back at all.

A grey dawn was breaking over the sea, a reassuring indication that Reub and Matthew had survived the night. Slowly the sky lightened with streaks of palest lemon and celadon green, then as the sun began its stately journey up towards the rim of the horizon, the low clouds became dramatically underlit with an angry, dark orange glow. Reub watched, tears of relief in his eyes, as a streak of fire broke the horizon and streamed over the sea towards them. It was hard to believe that, whilst they had spent frightening hours in the pitch dark, the comforting sun had been shining all the time on the other side of the world.

From where they sat, huddled on the upturned wrecked hull, level with the surface of the sea, it appeared as if the sun was forcing itself out of the water, bursting into a glowing orb of such flaming brightness he could no longer watch it. It was the most beautiful sight he had ever seen. Even the spectacular dawns he had witnessed in the tropics were nothing like this. Of course, he was affected by the emotion that he had survived, and overcome with sadness that as yet he knew nothing of the fates of Zack, Sandy and Isaac. He felt guilty that Matthew was having to endure all this, and tried not to think about Damaris and little Ben waiting for him at home. He was thankful that they were unaware of what he was suffering.

At first light, Reuben and Matthew strained their eyes looking for any sign of life. Among the distant floating debris they spotted one of their cobles, still afloat but drifting helplessly without oars. An arm waved feebly. It looked like Sandy, so perhaps there was still hope that he and Isaac were still alive. Of Zack there was still no sign.

On the clearing horizon they saw a most welcome sight. One of the five-man boats from Bay was slowly sailing towards them. They waved frantically, and watched with relief as the boat came alongside and took the small coble in tow. The sails filled, and the little convoy sailed on towards the *Elizabeth*. As they drew near, Reub and Matt could see that Sandy looked fit and well though still very wet. Isaac, however, was lying in the bottom of the coble with a bandage round a bleeding head wound, stirring restlessly and trying to say something.

'Ah dean't knaw what he's mutterin' aboot,' reported Sandy, in an undertone to Reub. 'Summat aboot buyin' a wind and undoin' knots in a rope. 'E's had a bad knock on t'ead. Must 'ave bashed 'im silly. Poor owd chap.' Sandy gently patted Isaac on the arm. 'Happen he'll mek sense when we get 'im home.'

Fortunately, for his peace of mind for ever after, Matthew never heard what Sandy had said.

Isaac never did recover his senses, and for the rest of his life was a pitiable figure, sitting by the slipway and telling anyone who would listen about how he had bought the wind that had nearly killed them all. Those who did not know of the superstition shook their heads and tapped their foreheads sadly. Those who *did* know regarded the pathetic old man with compassion.

The boat that came to the rescue belonged to one of the Storms' rivals in the fishing trade. There were always petty feuds going on between various families. Sometimes these burst into full-blown quarrels and fights, sometimes they just simmered on with barely concealed unpleasantness. In times of trouble, however, feuds were put aside.

Even so, Reub felt a degree of chagrin when he saw who his rescuers were, but was so relieved that he welcomed them with a wave and a cheerful grin, and refused to rise to the baited comments. His rivals had also experienced the storm, but had been on the edge and survived with nothing more than a bit of lost equipment.

It was not going to be easy to transfer the semi-consciuos Isaac into the rescue boat, so Sandy agreed to stay with him and be towed behind in the coble.

They were all skilled mariners and, having looked over the upturned hull in daylight, could see no obviously serious damage. It was impossible to right the boat, so after taking Reub and Matthew on board, they secured a tow-rope to the *Elizabeth*, hoisted their sails, and the sad little convoy began the long journey home.

Reub and Matt dreaded their homecoming. What would they tell Liz? Would they have the heart to pick up the pieces and start again? Once more, their future was uncertain.

It was a cold morning early in November when William Barnard decided to take a walk before breakfast to check on the fences of his cliff-edge field. Frequently after heavy rain, the soft clay slipped down to the beach, taking with it parts of the fences that kept his sheep from falling over. It was a regular and necessary part of the general farm maintenance.

William enjoyed these early morning walks with his dog. Although it was cold, the air was fresh and clear, and the early-morning mists which had dewed the late leaves and spangled the cobwebs with a million dewdrops charged the landscape with a special kind of magic.

William finished his inspection. The damage this time was not too bad, and repairs could wait a little longer. He paused, leaning on the gate which led to the track down to the shore. The sun was coming up over the sea; it was going to be a beautiful morning. Soon he would turn for home where Jane would have his breakfast on the table, and his three well-scrubbed and shiny-faced children would be waiting for him. He was a very lucky man, he knew, and he never forgot his good fortune.

Glancing down to where the tide was now beginning to lap at the foot of the cliff, he observed a dark blue bundle rolling in the surf. He had a horrible premonition that he knew what it was, though who, and where he was from, would be determined later.

Commanding his dog to 'stay!' William scrambled down the rough track, his heart beating in his chest. He knew that what he found would make him feel very sick.

Reluctantly, he approached the body and gently hauled it to the shore. Turning it over with his foot, he saw that, whoever it was, the sea had not been kind to him for the body was completely unrecognisable from its submersion in the water and the battering of the rocks. He knelt down beside it and struggled to open the toggles on the saturated pea-jacket. He hated doing this, afraid of what he would find.

With a sense of horrified disbelief he recognised the pattern on the knitted gansey as belonging to the Storm family of Robin Hood's Bay.

'Oh, please God, no!' he exclaimed silently.

Which one could it be? Surely not young Matthew who had so much life ahead of him, and please, please, don't let it be Reuben. Reuben who had suffered so much, and had now come home to re-make his life with his lovely young wife and his small son.

William drew a deep breath to calm himself, then carefully lifted the hem of the gansey, and brushed away the clinging sand and weed.

It looked very much like he was going to be the bearer of sad news to the poor man's unsuspecting widow. No way could he go home and face his breakfast - in fact he wondered how he was going to get through the rest of the day after he had made his visit to Liz, for clearly, in the plain part above the welt had been knitted the initials 'Z S'.

William gently dragged the body clear of the incoming tide and went to the village for help in bringing the old fisherman home.

The sea, from which Zachariah Storm had taken his living, had claimed its final payment.

# Epilogue

Although this story and 'For a Keg of Good Brandy' follow the fortunes of the fictitious 'Storm' family, the real-life Storms were one of the major fishing families of Robin Hood's Bay for generations. There were many branches of the family, most of whom, but not all, depended on the sea for a living. Many of them became Master Mariners, and today there are descendants of the Robin Hood's Bay Storms in many parts of the world.

They, like their contemporaries were tough and resilient. They had to be to survive.

By the end of the nineteenth century only eight working fishermen remained - four of these were the indestructible Storms - two of them were aged 83 and 85!

Another Storm was the last real full-time fisherman to bring his boat ashore for the last time at the end of the Second World War.

For the fishing Storms and others of their generation,
the Tide had truly Ebbed.